NIGHT of the
LIVING DUMMY 2

NIGHT of the LIVING DUMMY 2

R.L. STINE

SCHOLASTIC

Scholastic Children's Books
An imprint of Scholastic Ltd
Euston House, 24 Eversholt Street, London, NW1 1DB, UK
Registered office: Westfield Road, Southam, Warwickshire, CV47 0RA
SCHOLASTIC, GOOSEBUMPS, GOOSEBUMPS HORRORLAND and
associated logos are trademarks and/or registered trademarks of Scholastic Inc.

First Published in the US by Scholastic Inc, 1995
First published in the UK by Scholastic Ltd, 1996
This edition published by Scholastic Ltd, 2015

ISBN 978 1407 15732 0

Goosebumps books created by Parachute Press, Inc.

A CIP catalogue record for this book
is available from the British Library.

Printed by CPI Group (UK) Ltd, Croydon, CR0 4YY
Papers used by Scholastic Children's Books are made
from wood grown in sustainable forests.

11

www.scholastic.co.uk

My name is Amy Kramer, and every Thursday night I feel a little dumb. That's because Thursday is "Family Sharing Night" at my house.

Sara and Jed think it's dumb, too. But Mom and Dad won't listen to our complaints. "It's the most important night of the week," Dad says.

"It's a family tradition," Mom adds. "It's something you kids will always remember."

Right, Mom. It's something I'll always remember as really painful and embarrassing.

You've probably guessed that on Family Sharing Night, every member of the Kramer family — except for George, our cat — has to share something with the rest of the family.

It isn't so bad for my sister, Sara. Sara is fourteen — two years older than me — and she's a genius painter. Really. One of her paintings was chosen for a show at the art museum downtown. Sara may go to a special arts high school next year.

So Sara always shares some sketches she's

working on. Or a new painting.

And Family Sharing Night isn't so bad for Jed, either. My ten-year-old brother is such a total goof. He doesn't care what he shares. One Thursday night, he burped really loud and explained that he was sharing his dinner.

Jed laughed like a lunatic.

But Mom and Dad didn't think it was funny. They gave Jed a stern lecture about taking Family Sharing Night more seriously.

The next Thursday night, my obnoxious brother shared a note that David Miller, a kid at my school, had written to me. A very personal note! Jed found the note in my room and decided to share it with everyone.

Nice?

I wanted to die. I really did.

Jed just thinks he's so cute and adorable, he can get away with anything. He thinks he's really special.

I think it's because he's the only redhead in the family. Sara and I both have straight black hair, dark green eyes, and very tan skin. With his pale skin, freckled face, and curly red hair, Jed looks like he comes from another family!

And sometimes Sara and I both wish he did.

Anyway, I'm the one with the most problems on Family Sharing Night. Because I'm not really talented the way Sara is. And I'm not a total goof like Jed.

So I never really know what to share.

I mean, I have a seashell collection, which I keep in a jar on my dresser. But it's really kind of boring to hold up shells and talk about them. And we haven't been to the ocean for nearly two years. So my shells are kind of old, and everyone has already seen them.

I also have a really good collection of CDs. But no one else in my family is into Bob Marley and reggae music. If I start to share some music with them, they all hold their ears and complain till I shut it off.

So I usually make up some kind of a story — an adventure story about a girl who survives danger after danger. Or a wild fairy tale about princesses who turn into tigers.

After my last story, Dad had a big smile on his face. "Amy is going to be a famous writer," he announced. "She's so good at making up stories." Dad gazed around the room, still smiling. "We have such a talented family!" he exclaimed.

I knew he was just saying that to be a good parent. To "encourage" me. Sara is the real talent in our family. Everyone knows that.

Tonight, Jed was the first to share. Mom and Dad sat on the living room couch. Dad had taken out a tissue and was squinting as he cleaned his glasses. Dad can't stand to have the tiniest speck of dust on his glasses. He cleans them about twenty times a day.

I settled in the big brown armchair against the wall. Sara sat cross-legged on the carpet

3

beside my chair.

"What are you going to share tonight?" Mom asked Jed. "And I hope it isn't another horrible burp."

"That was so gross!" Sara moaned.

"Your face is gross!" Jed shot back. He stuck out his tongue at Sara.

"Jed, please — give us a break tonight," Dad muttered, slipping his glasses back on, adjusting them on his nose. "Don't cause trouble."

"She started it," Jed insisted, pointing at Sara.

"Just share something," I told Jed, sighing.

"I'm going to share your freckles," Sara told him. "I'm going to pull them off one by one and feed them to George."

Sara and I laughed. George didn't glance up. He was curled up, napping on the carpet beside the couch.

"That's not funny, girls," Mom snapped. "Stop being mean to your brother."

"This is supposed to be a family night," Dad wailed. "Why can't we be a family?"

"We are!" Jed insisted.

Dad frowned and shook his head. He looks like an owl when he does that. "Jed, are you going to share something?" he demanded weakly.

Jed nodded. "Yeah." He stood in the center of the room and shoved his hands into his jeans pockets. He wears loose, baggy jeans about ten

4

sizes too big. They always look as if they're about to fall down. Jed thinks that's cool.

"I . . . uh . . . learned to whistle through my fingers," he announced.

"Wow," Sara muttered sarcastically.

Jed ignored her. He pulled his hands from his pockets. Then he stuck his two little fingers into the sides of his mouth — and let out a long, shrill whistle.

He whistled through his fingers two more times. Then he took a deep bow. The whole family burst into loud applause.

Jed, grinning, took another low bow.

"Such a talented family!" Dad declared. This time, he meant it as a joke.

Jed dropped down on the floor beside George, startling the poor cat awake.

"Your turn next, Amy," Mom said, turning to me. "Are you going to tell us another story?"

"Her stories are too long!" Jed complained.

George climbed unsteadily to his feet and moved a few feet away from Jed. Yawning, the cat dropped onto his stomach beside Mom's feet.

"I'm not going to tell a story tonight," I announced. I picked up Dennis from behind my armchair.

Sara and Jed both groaned.

"Hey — give me a break!" I shouted. I settled back on the edge of the chair, fixing my dummy on my lap. "I thought I'd talk to Dennis tonight," I told Mom and Dad.

5

They had half-smiles on their faces. I didn't care. I'd been practicing with Dennis all week. And I wanted to try out my new comedy routine with him.

"Amy is a lousy ventriloquist," Jed chimed in. "You can see her lips move."

"Be quiet, Jed. I think Dennis is funny," Sara said. She scooted toward the couch so she could see better.

I balanced Dennis on my left knee and wrapped my fingers around the string in his back that worked his mouth. Dennis is a very old ventriloquist's dummy. The paint on his face is faded. One eye is almost completely white. His turtleneck sweater is torn and tattered.

But I have a lot of fun with him. When my five-year-old cousins come to visit, I like to entertain them with Dennis. They squeal and laugh. They think I'm a riot.

I think I'm getting much better with Dennis. Despite Jed's complaints.

I took a deep breath, glanced at Mom and Dad, and began my act.

"How are you tonight, Dennis?" I asked.

"*Not too well*," I made the dummy reply in a high, shrill voice. Dennis's voice.

"Really, Dennis? What's wrong?"

"*I think I caught a bug.*"

"You mean you have the flu?" I asked him.

"*No. Termites!*"

Mom and Dad laughed. Sara smiled. Jed

6

groaned loudly.

I turned back to Dennis. "Well, have you been to a doctor?" I asked him.

"No. A carpenter!"

Mom and Dad smiled at that one, but didn't laugh. Jed groaned again. Sara stuck her finger down her throat, pretending to puke.

"No one liked that joke, Dennis," I told him.

"Who's joking?" I made Dennis reply.

"This is lame," I heard Jed mutter to Sara. She nodded her head in agreement.

"Let's change the subject, Dennis," I said, shifting the dummy to my other knee. "Do you have a girlfriend?"

I leaned Dennis forward, trying to make him nod his head yes. But his head rolled right off his shoulders.

The wooden head hit the floor with a *thud* and bounced over to George. The cat leaped up and scampered away.

Sara and Jed collapsed in laughter, slapping each other high fives.

I jumped angrily to my feet. "Dad!" I screamed. "You *promised* you'd buy me a new dummy!"

Jed scurried over to the rug and picked up Dennis's head. He pulled the string, making the dummy's mouth move. "Amy reeks! Amy reeks!" Jed made the dummy repeat over and over.

"Give me that!" I grabbed the head angrily

7

from Jed's hand.

"Amy reeks! Amy reeks!" Jed continued chanting.

"That's enough!" Mom shouted, jumping up off the couch.

Jed retreated back to the wall.

"I've been checking the stores for a new dummy," Dad told me, pulling off his glasses again and examining them closely. "But they're all so expensive."

"Well, how am I ever going to get better at this?" I demanded. "Dennis's head falls off every time I use him!"

"Do your best," Mom said.

What did *that* mean? I always hated it when she said that.

"Instead of Family Sharing Night, we should call this the Thursday Night Fights," Sara declared.

Jed raised his fists. "Want to fight?" he asked Sara.

"It's your turn, Sara," Mom replied, narrowing her eyes at Jed. "What are you sharing tonight?"

"I have a new painting," Sara announced. "It's a watercolor."

"Of what?" Dad asked, settling his glasses back on his face.

"Remember that cabin we had in Maine a few summers ago?" Sara replied, tossing back her straight black hair. "The one overlooking the dark rock cliff? I found a snapshot of it, and I tried to paint it."

I suddenly felt really angry and upset. I admit it. I was jealous of Sara.

Here she was, about to share another beautiful watercolor. And here I was, rolling a stupid wooden dummy head in my lap.

It just wasn't fair!

"You'll have to come to my room to see it," Sara was saying. "It's still wet."

We all stood up and trooped to Sara's room.

My family lives in a long, one-story, ranch-style house. My room and Jed's room are at the end of one hallway. The living room, dining room, and kitchen are in the middle. Sara's room and my parents' room are down the other hall, way at the other end of the house.

I led the way down the hall. Behind me, Sara was going on and on about all the trouble she'd had with the painting and how she'd solved the problems.

"I remember that cabin so well," Dad said.

"I can't wait to see the painting," Mom added.

I stepped into Sara's room and clicked on the light.

Then I turned to the easel by the window that held the painting — and let out a scream of horror.

My mouth dropped open in shock. I stared at the painting, unable to speak.

When Sara saw it, she let out a shriek. "I — I don't *believe* it!" she screamed. "Who *did* that?"

Someone had painted a yellow-and-black smiley face in the corner of her painting. Right in the middle of the black rock cliff.

Mom and Dad stepped up to the easel, fretful expressions on their faces. They studied the smiley face, then turned to Jed.

Jed burst out laughing. "Do you like it?" he asked innocently.

"Jed — how *could* you!" Sara exploded. "I'll kill you! I really will!"

"The painting was too dark," Jed explained with a shrug. "I wanted to brighten it up."

"But . . . but . . . but . . ." my sister sputtered. She balled her hands into fists, shook them at Jed, and uttered a loud cry of rage.

"Jed — what were you doing in Sara's room?" Mom demanded.

Sara doesn't like for anyone to go into her precious room without a written invitation!

"Young man, you know you're never allowed to touch your sister's paintings," Dad scolded.

"I can paint, too," Jed replied. "I'm a good painter."

"Then do your own paintings!" Sara snapped. "Don't sneak in here and mess up my work!"

"I didn't sneak," Jed insisted. He sneered at Sara. "I was just trying to help."

"You were not!" Sara screamed, angrily tossing her black hair over her shoulder. "You ruined my painting!"

"Your painting reeks!" Jed shot back.

"Enough!" Mom shouted. She grabbed Jed by both shoulders. "Jed — look at me! You don't seem to see how serious this is. This is the worst thing you've ever done!"

Jed's smile finally faded.

I took another glance at the ugly smiley face he had slopped on to Sara's watercolor. Since he's the baby in the family, Jed thinks he can get away with anything.

But I knew that this time he had gone too far.

After all, Sara is the star of the family. She's the talented one. The one with the painting that hung in a museum. Messing with Sara's precious painting was bound to get Jed in major trouble.

Sara is so stuck-up about her paintings. A few times, I even thought about painting something funny on one of them. But of course I only *thought* it. I would *never* do anything that horrible.

"You don't have to be jealous of your sister's work," Dad was telling Jed. "We're all talented in this family."

"Oh, sure," Jed muttered. He has this weird habit. Whenever he's in trouble, he doesn't say he's sorry. Instead, he gets really angry. "What's *your* talent, Dad?" Jed demanded, sneering.

Dad's jaw tightened. He narrowed his eyes at Jed. "We're not discussing me," he said in a low voice. "But I'll tell you. My talent is my Chinese cooking. There are all kinds of talents, Jed."

Dad considers himself a Master of the Wok. Once or twice a week, he chops a ton of vegetables into little pieces and fries them up in the electric wok Mom got him for Christmas.

We pretend it tastes great.

No point in hurting Dad's feelings.

"Is Jed going to be punished or not?" Sara demanded in a shrill voice.

She had opened her box of watercolor paints and was rolling a brush in the black. Then she began painting over the smiley face with quick, furious strokes.

"Yes, Jed is going to be punished," Mom replied, glaring at him. Jed lowered his eyes to the floor. "First he's going to apologize to Sara."

We all waited.

It took Jed a while. But he finally managed

12

to mutter, "Sorry, Sara."

He started to leave the room, but Mom grabbed his shoulders again and pulled him back. "Not so fast, Jed," she told him. "Your punishment is you can't go to the movies with Josh and Matt on Saturday. And . . . no video games for a week."

"Mom — give me a break!" Jed whined.

"What you did was really bad," Mom said sternly. "Maybe this punishment will make you realize how horrible it was."

"But I *have* to go to the movies!" Jed protested.

"You can't," Mom replied softly. "And no arguing, or I'll add on to your punishment. Now go to your room."

"I don't think it's enough punishment," Sara said, dabbing away at her painting.

"Keep out of it, Sara," Mom snapped.

"Yeah. Keep out of it," Jed muttered. He stomped out of the room and down the long hall to his room.

Dad sighed. He swept a hand back over his bald head. "Family Sharing Night is over," he said sadly.

I stayed in Sara's room and watched her repair the painting for a while. She kept tsk-tsking and shaking her head.

"I have to make the rocks much darker, or the paint won't cover the stupid smiley face," she

13

explained unhappily. "But if I make the rocks darker, I have to change the sky. The whole balance is ruined."

"I think it looks pretty good," I told her, trying to cheer her up.

"How could Jed do that?" Sara demanded, dipping her brush in the water jar. "How could he sneak in here and totally destroy a work of art?"

I was feeling sorry for Sara. But that remark made me lose all sympathy. I mean, why couldn't she just call it a watercolor painting? Why did she have to call it "a work of art"?

Sometimes she is so stuck-up and so in love with herself, it makes me sick.

I turned and left the room. She didn't even notice.

I went down the hall to my room and called my friend Margo. We talked for a while about stuff. And we made plans to get together the next day.

As I talked on the phone, I could hear Jed in his room next door. He was pacing back and forth, tossing things around, making a lot of noise.

Sometimes I spell the word *Jed* B-R-A-T.

Margo's dad made her get off the phone. He's real strict. He never lets her talk for more than ten or fifteen minutes.

I wandered into the kitchen and made myself a bowl of Frosted Flakes. My favorite late snack. When I was a little kid, I used to have a bowl of cereal every night before bed. And I just never got out of the habit.

I rinsed out the bowl. Then I said good night to Mom and Dad and went to bed.

It was a warm spring night. A soft breeze fluttered the curtains over the window. Pale light from a big half-moon filled the window and spilled onto the floor.

I fell into a deep sleep as soon as my head hit the pillow.

A short while later, something woke me up. I'm not sure what.

Still half asleep, I blinked my eyes open and raised myself on my pillow. I struggled to see clearly.

The curtains flapped over the window.

I felt as if I were still asleep, dreaming.

But what I saw in the window snapped me awake.

The curtains billowed, then lifted away.

And in the silvery light, I saw a face.

An ugly, grinning face in my bedroom window. Staring through the darkness at me.

The curtains flapped again.

The face didn't move.

"Who?" I choked out, squeezing the sheet up to my chin.

The eyes stared in at me. Cold, unblinking eyes.

Dummy eyes.

Dennis.

Dennis stared blankly at me, his white eye catching the glow of the moonlight.

I let out an angry roar, tossed off the sheet, and bolted out of bed. To the window.

I pushed away the billowing curtains and grabbed Dennis's head off the window ledge. "Who put you there?" I demanded, holding the head between my hands. "Who did it, Dennis?"

I heard soft laughter behind me. From the hallway.

I flew across the room, the head still in my hands. I pulled open my bedroom door.

Jed held his hand over his mouth, muffling his

laughter. "Gotcha!" he whispered gleefully.

"Jed — you creep!" I cried. I let the dummy head drop to the floor. Then I grabbed Jed's pajama pants with both hands and jerked them up as high as I could — nearly to his chin!

He let out a gasp of pain and stumbled back against the wall.

"Why did you do that?" I demanded in an angry whisper. "Why did you put the dummy head on my window ledge?"

Jed tugged his pajama pants back into place. "To pay you back," he muttered.

"Huh? Me?" I shrieked. "I didn't do anything to you. What did *I* do?"

"You didn't stick up for me," he grumbled, scratching his red curly hair. His eyes narrowed at me. "You didn't say anything to help me out. You know. About Sara's painting."

"Excuse me?" I cried. "How could I help you out? What could I say?"

"You could have said it was no big deal," Jed replied.

"But it *was* a big deal!" I told him. "You know how seriously Sara takes her paintings." I shook my head. "I'm sorry, Jed. But you deserve to be punished. You really do."

He stared at me across the dim hallway, thinking about what I'd said. Then an evil smile spread slowly over his freckled face. "Hope I didn't scare you too much, Amy." He snickered. Then he picked Dennis's head up off the carpet

17

and tossed it at me.

I caught it in one hand. "Go to sleep, Jed," I told him. "And don't mess with Dennis again!"

I stepped back into my room and closed the door. I tossed Dennis's head onto a pile of clothes on my desk chair. Then I climbed wearily back into bed.

So much trouble around here tonight, I thought, shutting my eyes, trying to relax.

So much trouble . . .

Two days later, Dad brought home a present for me.

A new ventriloquist's dummy.

That's when the *real* trouble began.

Margo came over the next afternoon. Margo is real tiny, sort of like a mini-person. She has a tiny face, and is very pretty, with bright blue eyes and delicate features.

Her blond hair is very light and very fine. She let it grow this year. It's just about down to her tiny little waist.

She's nearly a foot shorter than me, even though we both turned twelve in February. She's very smart and very popular. But the boys like to make fun of her soft, whispery voice.

Today she was wearing a bright blue tank top tucked into white tennis shorts. "I bought the new Beatles collection," she told me as she stepped into the house. She held up a CD box.

Margo loves the Beatles. She doesn't listen to any of the new groups. She has all of the Beatles albums. And she has Beatles posters on the walls in her room.

We went to my room and put on the CD. Margo settled on the bed. I sprawled on the carpet across from her.

"My dad almost didn't let me come over," Margo told me, pushing her long hair behind her shoulder. "He thought he might need me to work at the restaurant."

Margo's dad owns a huge restaurant downtown called The Party House. It's not really a restaurant. It's a big, old house filled with enormous rooms where people can hold parties.

A lot of kids have birthday parties there. And there are bar mitzvahs and confirmations and wedding receptions there, too. Sometimes there are six parties going on at once!

One Beatles song ended. The next song, "Love Me Do," started up.

"I *love* this song!" Margo exclaimed. She sang along with it for a while. I tried singing with her, but I'm totally tone deaf. As my dad says, I can't carry a tune in a wheelbarrow.

"Well, I'm glad you didn't have to work today," I told Margo.

"Me, too," Margo sighed. "Dad always gives me the worst jobs. You know. Clearing tables. Or putting away dishes. Or wrapping up garbage bags. Yuck."

She started singing again — and then stopped. She sat up on the bed. "Amy, I almost forgot. Dad may have a job for you."

"Excuse me?" I replied. "Wrapping up garbage bags? I don't think so, Margo."

"No. No. Listen," Margo pleaded excitedly in

her mouselike voice. "It's a good job. Dad has a bunch of birthday parties coming up. For teeny tiny kids. You know. Two-year-olds. Maybe three- or four-year-olds. And he thought you could entertain them."

"Huh?" I stared at my friend. I still didn't understand. "You mean, sing or something?"

"No. With Dennis," Margo explained. She twisted a lock of hair around in her fingers and bobbed her head in time to the music as she talked. "Dad saw you with Dennis at the sixth-grade talent night. He was really impressed."

"He was? I was terrible that night!" I replied.

"Well, Dad didn't think so. He wonders if you'd like to come to the birthday parties and put on a show with Dennis. The little kids will love it. Dad said he'd even pay you."

"Wow! That's cool!" I replied. What an exciting idea.

Then I remembered something.

I jumped to my feet, crossed the room to the chair, and held up Dennis's head. "One small problem," I groaned.

Margo let go of her hair and made a sick face. "His head? Why did you take off his head?"

"I didn't," I replied. "It fell off. Every time I use Dennis, his head falls off."

"Oh." Margo uttered a disappointed sigh. "The head looks weird all by itself. I don't think little kids would like it if it fell off."

"I don't think so," I agreed.

"It might frighten them or something," Margo said. "You know. Give them nightmares. Make them think their own head might fall off."

"Dennis is totally wrecked. Dad promised me a new dummy. But he hasn't been able to find one."

"Too bad," Margo replied. "You'd have fun performing for the kids."

We listened to more Beatles music. Then Margo had to go home.

A few minutes after she left, I heard the front door slam.

"Hey, Amy! Amy — are you home?" I heard Dad call from the living room.

"Coming!" I called. I made my way to the front of the house. Dad stood in the entryway, a long carton under his arm, a smile on his face.

He handed the carton to me. "Happy Un-birthday!" he exclaimed.

"Dad! Is it?" I cried. I tore open the carton. "Yes!" A new dummy!

I lifted him carefully out of the carton.

The dummy had wavy brown hair painted on top of his wooden head. I studied his face. It was kind of strange. Kind of intense. His eyes were bright blue — not faded like Dennis's. He had bright red painted lips, curved up into an eerie smile. His lower lip had a chip on one side so that it didn't quite match the other lip.

As I pulled him from the box, the dummy appeared to stare into my eyes. The eyes sparkled. The grin grew wider.

I felt a sudden chill. *Why does this dummy seem to be laughing at me?* I wondered.

I held him up, examining him carefully. He wore a gray, double-breasted suit over a white shirt collar. The collar was stapled to his neck. He didn't have a shirt. Instead, his wooden chest had been painted white.

Big, black leather shoes were attached to the ends of his thin, dangling legs.

"Dad — he's great!" I exclaimed.

"I found him in a pawnshop," Dad said, picking up the dummy's hand and pretending to shake hands with it. "How do you do, Slappy?"

"Slappy? Is that his name?"

"That's what the man in the store said," Dad replied. He lifted Slappy's arms, examining his suit. "I don't know why he sold Slappy so cheaply. He practically *gave* the dummy away!"

I turned the dummy around and looked for the string in his back that made the mouth open and close. "He's excellent, Dad," I said. I kissed my dad on the cheek. "Thanks."

"Do you really like him?" Dad asked.

Slappy grinned up at me. His blue eyes stared into mine. He seemed to be waiting for an answer, too.

"Yes. He's awesome!" I said. "I like his serious eyes. They look so real."

"The eyes move," Dad said. "They're not painted on like Dennis's. They don't blink, but they move from side to side."

I reached my hand inside the dummy's back. "How do you make his eyes move?" I asked.

"The man showed me," Dad said. "It's not hard. First you grab the string that works the mouth."

"I've got that," I told him.

"Then you move your hand up into the dummy's head. There is a little lever up there. Do you feel it? Push on it. The eyes will move in the direction you push."

"Okay. I'll try," I said.

Slowly I moved my hand up inside the dummy's back. Through the neck. And into his head.

I stopped and let out a startled cry as my hand hit something soft.

Something soft and warm.

His brain!

"Ohhh." I uttered a sick moan and jerked my hand out as fast as I could.

I could still feel the soft, warm mush on my fingers.

"Amy — what's wrong?" Dad cried.

"His — his brains!" I choked out, feeling my stomach lurch.

"Huh? What are you *talking* about?" Dad grabbed the dummy from my hands. He turned it over and reached into the back.

I covered my mouth with both hands and watched him reach into the head. His eyes widened in surprise.

He struggled with something. Then pulled his hand out.

"Yuck!" I groaned. "What's *that*?"

Dad stared down at the mushy, green and purple and brown object in his hand. "Looks like someone left a sandwich in there!" he exclaimed.

Dad's whole face twisted in disgust. "It's all

moldy and rotten. Must have been in there for months!"

"Yuck!" I repeated, holding my nose. "It really stinks! Why would someone leave a sandwich in a dummy's head?"

"Beats me," Dad replied, shaking his head. "And it looks like there are wormholes in it!"

"Yuuuuuck!" we both cried in unison.

Dad handed Slappy back to me. Then he hurried into the kitchen to get rid of the rotted, moldy sandwich.

I heard him run the garbage disposal. Then I heard water running as he washed his hands. A few seconds later, Dad returned to the living room, drying his hands on a dish towel.

"Maybe we'd better examine Slappy closely," he suggested. "We don't want any more surprises — *do* we!"

I carried Slappy into the kitchen, and we stretched him out on the counter. Dad examined the dummy's shoes carefully. They were attached to the legs and didn't come off.

I put my finger on the dummy's chin and moved the mouth up and down. Then I checked out his wooden hands.

I unbuttoned the gray suit jacket and studied the dummy's painted shirt. Patches of the white paint had chipped and cracked. But it was okay.

"Everything looks fine, Dad," I reported.

He nodded. Then he smelled his fingers. I guess he hadn't washed away all of the stink

26

from the rotted sandwich.

"We'd better spray the inside of his head with disinfectant or perfume or something," Dad said.

Then, as I was buttoning up the jacket, something caught my eye.

Something yellow. A slip of paper poking up from the jacket pocket.

It's probably a sales receipt, I thought.

But when I pulled out the small square of yellow paper, I found strange writing on it. Weird words in a language I'd never seen before.

I squinted hard at the paper and slowly read the words out loud:

"Karru marri odonna loma molonu karrano."

I wonder what that means? I thought.

And then I glanced down at Slappy's face.

And saw his red lips twitch.

And saw one eye slowly close in a wink.

"D-D-Dad!" I stuttered. "He — moved!"

"Huh?" Dad had gone back to the sink to wash his hands for a third time. "What's wrong with the dummy?"

"He moved!" I cried. "He *winked* at me!"

Dad came over to the counter, wiping his hands. "I told you, Amy — he can't blink. The eyes only move from side to side."

"No!" I insisted. "He winked. His lips twitched, and he winked."

Dad frowned and picked up the dummy head in both hands. He raised it to examine it. "Well . . . maybe the eyelids are loose," he said. "I'll see if I can tighten them up. Maybe if I take a screwdriver I can —"

Dad didn't finish his sentence.

Because the dummy swung his wooden hand up and hit Dad on the side of the head.

"Ow!" Dad cried, dropping the dummy back onto the counter. Dad grabbed his cheek. "Hey — stop it, Amy! That hurt!"

"Me?" I shrieked. "I didn't do it!"

Dad glared at me, rubbing his cheek. It had turned bright red.

"The dummy did it!" I insisted. "I didn't touch him, Dad! I didn't move his hand!"

"Not funny," Dad muttered. "You know I don't like practical jokes."

I opened my mouth to answer, but no words came out. I decided I'd better just shut up.

Of course Dad wouldn't believe that the dummy had slapped him.

I didn't believe it myself.

Dad must have pulled too hard when he was examining the head. Dad jerked the hand up without realizing it.

That's how I explained it to myself.

What other explanation could there be?

I apologized to Dad. Then we washed Slappy's face with a damp sponge. We cleaned him up and sprayed disinfectant inside his head.

He was starting to look pretty good.

I thanked Dad again and hurried to my room. I set Slappy down on the chair beside Dennis. Then I phoned Margo.

"I got a new dummy," I told her excitedly. "I can perform for the kids' birthday parties. At The Party House."

"That's great, Amy!" Margo exclaimed. "Now all you need is an act."

She was right.

I needed jokes. A lot of jokes. If I was going to perform with Slappy in front of dozens of kids, I needed a long comedy act.

The next day after school, I hurried to the library. I took out every joke book I could find. I carried them home and studied them. I wrote down all the jokes I thought I could use with Slappy.

After dinner, I should have been doing my homework. Instead, I practiced with Slappy. I sat in front of the mirror and watched myself with him.

I tried hard to speak clearly but not move my lips. And I tried hard to move Slappy's mouth so that it really looked as if he were talking.

Working his mouth and moving his eyes at the same time was pretty hard. But after a while, it became easier.

I tried some knock-knock jokes with Slappy. I thought little kids might like those.

"Knock knock," I made Slappy say.

"Who's there?" I asked him, staring into his eyes as if I were really talking to him.

"Jane," Slappy said.

"Jane who?"

"Jane jer clothes. You stink!"

I practiced each joke over and over, watching myself in the mirror. I wanted to be a really good ventriloquist. I wanted to be excellent. I wanted to be as good with Slappy as Sara is with her paints.

I practiced some more knock-knock jokes and some jokes about animals. Jokes I thought little kids would find funny.

I'll try them out on Family Sharing Night, I decided. It will make Dad happy to see how hard I'm working with Slappy. At least I know Slappy's head won't fall off.

I glanced across the room at Dennis. He looked so sad and forlorn, crumpled in the chair, his head tilted nearly sideways on his shoulders.

Then I propped Slappy up and turned back to the mirror.

"Knock knock."

"Who's there?"

"Wayne."

"Wayne who?"

"Wayne wayne, go away! Come again another day!"

On Thursday night, I was actually eager to finish dinner so that Sharing Night could begin. I couldn't wait to show my family my new act with Slappy.

We had spaghetti for dinner. I like spaghetti, but Jed always ruins it.

He's so gross. He sat across the table from me, and he kept opening his mouth wide, showing me a mouth full of chewed-up spaghetti.

Then he'd laugh because he cracks himself up. And spaghetti sauce would run down his chin.

By the time dinner was over, Jed had spaghetti sauce smeared all over his face and all over the tablecloth around his plate.

No one seemed to notice. Mom and Dad were too busy listening to Sara brag about her grades. For a change.

Report cards were being handed out tomorrow. Sara was sure she was getting all A's.

I was sure, too. Sure I *wasn't* getting all A's!

I'd be lucky to get a C in math. I really messed up the last two tests. And I probably wasn't going to do real well in science, either. My weather balloon project fell apart, so I hadn't handed it in yet.

I finished my spaghetti and mopped up some of the leftover sauce on my plate with a chunk of bread.

When I glanced up, Jed had stuck two carrot sticks in his nose. "Amy, check this out. I'm a walrus!" he cried, grinning. He let out a few *urk urks* and clapped his hands together like a walrus.

"Jed — stop that!" Mom cried sharply. She made a disgusted face. "Get those out of your nose."

"Make him eat them, Mom!" I cried.

Jed stuck his tongue out at me. It was orange from the spaghetti sauce.

"Look at you. You're a mess!" Mom shouted at Jed. "Go get cleaned up. Now! Hurry! Wash all that sauce off your face."

Jed groaned. But he climbed to his feet and headed to the bathroom.

"Did he eat anything? Or did he just rub it all over himself?" Dad asked, rolling his eyes. Dad had some sauce on his chin, too, but I didn't say anything.

"You interrupted me," Sara said impatiently. "I was telling you about the State Art Contest. Remember? I sent my flower painting in for that?"

"Oh, yes," Mom replied. "Have you heard from the judges?"

I didn't listen to Sara's reply. My mind wandered. I started thinking again about how bad my report card was going to be. I had to force myself to stop thinking about it.

"Uh . . . I'll clear the dishes," I announced.

I started to stand up.

But I stopped with a startled cry when I saw the short figure creep into the living room.

A dummy!

My dummy.

He was crawling across the room!

I let out another cry. I pointed to the living room with a trembling finger. "M-Mom! Dad!" I stammered.

Sara was still talking about the art competition. But she turned to see what everyone was gaping at.

The dummy's head popped out from behind the armchair.

"It's Dennis!" I cried.

I heard muffled laughter. Jed's muffled laughter.

The dummy reached up both hands and pulled off his own head. And Jed's head popped up through the green turtleneck. He still had spaghetti sauce smeared on his cheeks. He was laughing hard.

Everyone else started to laugh, too. Everyone but me.

Jed had really frightened me.

He had pulled the neck of his sweater way up over his head. Then he had tucked Dennis's

34

wooden head inside the turtleneck.

Jed was so short and thin. It really looked as if Dennis were creeping into the room.

"Stop laughing!" I shouted at my family. "It isn't funny!"

"I think it's *very* funny!" Mom cried. "What a crazy thing to think of!"

"Very clever," Dad added.

"It's not clever," I insisted. I glared furiously at my brother. "I always knew you were a dummy!" I screamed at him.

"Amy, you really were scared," Sara accused. "You nearly dropped your teeth!"

"Not true!" I sputtered. "I knew it was Dennis — I mean — Jed!"

Now everyone started laughing at *me*! I could feel my face getting hot, and I knew I was blushing.

That made them all laugh even harder.

Nice family, huh?

I climbed to my feet, walked around the table, and took Dennis's head away from Jed. "Don't go in my room," I told him through clenched teeth. "And don't mess with my stuff." I stomped away to put the dummy head back in my room.

"It was just a joke, Amy," I heard Sara call after me.

"Yeah. It was just a joke," Jed repeated nastily.

"Ha-ha!" I shouted back at them. "What a riot!"

My anger had faded away by the time we started Family Sharing Night. We settled in the living room, taking our usual places.

Mom volunteered to go first. She told a funny story about something that had happened at work.

Mom works in a fancy women's clothing store downtown. She told us about a really big woman who came into the store and insisted on trying on only tiny sizes.

The woman ripped every piece of clothing she tried on — and then bought them all! "They're not for me," the woman explained. "They're for my sister!"

We all laughed. But I was surprised Mom told that story. Because Mom is pretty chubby. And she's very sensitive about it.

About as sensitive as Dad is about being bald.

Dad was the next to share. He brought out his guitar, and we all groaned. Dad thinks he's a great singer. But he's nearly as tone deaf as I am.

He loves singing all these old folk songs from the sixties. There's supposed to be some kind of message in them. But Sara, Jed, and I have no idea what he's singing about.

Dad strummed away and sang something about not working on Maggie's farm anymore. At least, I *think* that's what he was saying.

We all clapped and cheered. But Dad knew we didn't really mean it.

It was Jed's turn next. But he insisted that he had already shared. "Dressing up like Dennis — that was it," he said.

No one wanted to argue with him. "Your turn, Amy," Mom said, leaning against Dad on the couch. Dad fiddled with his glasses, then settled back.

I picked up Slappy and arranged him on my lap. I was feeling a little nervous. I wanted to do a good job and impress them with my new comedy act.

I'd been practicing all week, and I knew the jokes by heart. But as I slipped my hand into Slappy's back and found the string, my stomach felt all fluttery.

I cleared my throat and began.

"This is Slappy, everyone," I said. "Slappy, say hi to my family."

"Hi to my family!" I made Slappy say. I made his eyes slide back and forth.

They all chuckled.

"This dummy is so much better!" Mom commented.

"But it's the same old ventriloquist," Sara said cruelly.

I glared at her.

"Just joking! Just joking!" my sister insisted.

"I think that dummy reeks," Jed chimed in.

"Give Amy a break," Dad said sharply. "Go ahead, Amy."

I cleared my throat again. It suddenly felt

very dry. "Slappy and I are going to tell some knock-knock jokes," I announced. I turned to face Slappy and made him turn his head to me. "Knock knock," I said.

"Knock it off!" came the harsh reply.

Slappy spun around to face my Mom. *"Hey — don't break the sofa, fatso!"* he rasped. *"Why don't you skip the French fries and have a salad once in a while?"*

"Huh?" Mom gasped in shock. "Amy —"

"Amy, that's not funny!" Dad cried angrily.

"What's your problem, baldy?" Slappy shouted. *"Is that your head — or are you hatching an ostrich egg on your neck?"*

"That's enough, Amy!" Dad cried, jumping to his feet. "Stop it — right now!"

"But — but — Dad!" I sputtered.

"Why don't you put an extra hole in your head and use it for a bowling ball?" Slappy screamed at Dad.

"Your jokes are horrible!" Mom exclaimed. "They're hurtful and insulting."

"It's not funny, Amy!" Dad fumed. "It's not funny to hurt people's feelings."

"But, Dad —" I replied. "I didn't say any of that! It wasn't me! It was Slappy! Really! I wasn't saying it! I wasn't!"

Slappy raised his head. His red-lipped grin appeared to spread. His blue eyes sparkled. *"Did I mention you are all ugly?"* he asked.

Everyone started shouting at once.

I stood up and dropped Slappy facedown on the armchair.

My legs were trembling. My entire body was shaking.

What's going on here? I asked myself. *I didn't say those things. I really didn't.*

But Slappy can't be talking on his own — can *he?*

Of course not, I realized.

But what did that mean? Did that mean I was saying those horrible, insulting things to my parents without even knowing it?

Mom and Dad stood side by side, staring at me angrily, demanding to know why I insulted them.

"Did you really think that was funny?" Mom asked. "Didn't you think it would hurt my feelings to call me fatso?"

Meanwhile, Jed was sprawled on his back in the middle of the floor, giggling like a moron.

He thought the whole thing was a riot.

Sara sat cross-legged against the wall, shaking her head, her black hair falling over her face. "You're in major trouble," she muttered. "What's your problem, Amy?"

I turned to Mom and Dad. My hands were balled into tight fists. I couldn't stop shaking.

"You've got to believe me!" I shrieked. "I didn't say those things! I really didn't!"

"Yeah. Right. Slappy is a baaad dude!" Jed chimed in, grinning.

"Everybody, just be quiet!" Dad screamed. His face turned bright red.

Mom squeezed his arm. She didn't like it when he got too angry or excited. I guess she worried he might totally explode or something.

Dad crossed his arms in front of his chest. I saw that he had a sweat stain on the chest of his polo shirt. His face was still red.

The room suddenly fell silent.

"Amy, we're *not* going to believe you," Dad said softly.

"But — but — but —"

He raised a hand to silence me.

"You're a wonderful storyteller, Amy," Dad continued. "You make up wonderful fantasies and fairy tales. But we're not going to believe this one. I'm sorry. We're not going to believe that your dummy spoke up on his own."

"But he *did*!" I screamed. I felt like bursting out in sobs. I bit my lip hard, trying to force them back.

Dad shook his head. "No, Slappy didn't insult us. You said those things, Amy. You did. And now I want you to apologize to your mother and me. Then I want you to take your dummy and go to your room."

There was no way they'd ever believe me. No way. I wasn't sure I believed it myself.

"Sorry," I muttered, still holding back the tears. "Really. I'm sorry."

With an unhappy sigh, I lifted Slappy off the chair. I carried him around the waist so that his arms and legs dangled toward the floor. "Good night," I said. I walked slowly toward my room.

"What about my turn?" I heard Sara ask.

"Sharing Night is over," Dad replied grumpily. "You two — get lost. Leave your mom and me alone."

Dad sounded really upset.

I didn't blame him.

I stepped into my room and closed the door behind me. Then I lifted Slappy up, holding him under the shoulders. I raised his face to mine.

His eyes seemed to stare into my face.

Such cold blue eyes, I thought.

His bright red lips curled up into that smirking grin. The smile suddenly seemed evil. Mocking.

As if Slappy were laughing at me.

But of course that was impossible. My wild

imagination was playing tricks on me, I decided.

Frightening tricks.

Slappy was just a dummy, after all. Just a hunk of painted wood.

I stared hard into those cold blue eyes. "Slappy, look at all the trouble you caused me tonight," I told him.

Thursday night had been awful. Totally awful.

But Friday turned out to be much worse.

First I dropped my tray in the lunchroom. The trays were all wet, and mine just slipped out of my hand.

The plates clattered on the floor, and my lunch spilled all over my new white sneakers. Everyone in the lunchroom clapped and cheered.

Was I embarrassed? Take three guesses.

Later that afternoon, report cards were handed out.

Sara came home grinning and singing. Nothing makes her more happy than being perfect. And her report card was perfect. All A's.

She insisted on showing it to me three times. She showed it to Jed three times, too. And we both had to tell her how wonderful she was each time.

I'm being unfair to Sara.

She was happy and excited. And she had a right to be. Her report card was perfect — *and* her flower painting won the blue ribbon in the State Art Contest.

So I shouldn't blame her for dancing around the house and singing at the top of her lungs.

She wasn't trying to rub it in. She wasn't trying to make me feel like a lowly slug because my report card had two C's. One in math and one in science.

It wasn't Sara's fault that I had received my worst report card ever.

So I tried to hold back my jealous feelings and not strangle her the tenth time she told me about the art prize. But it wasn't easy.

The worst part of my report card wasn't the two C's. It was the little note Miss Carson wrote at the bottom.

It said: *Amy isn't working to the best of her ability. If she worked harder, she could do much better than this.*

I don't think teachers should be allowed to write notes on report cards. I think getting grades is bad enough.

I tried to make up some kind of story to explain the two C's to my parents. I planned to tell them that *everyone* in the class got C's in math and science. "Miss Carson didn't have time to grade our papers. So she gave us all C's — just to be fair."

It was a good story. But not a great story.

No way Mom and Dad would buy that one.

I paced back and forth in my room, trying to think of a better story. After a while, I noticed Slappy staring at me.

44

He sat in the chair beside Dennis, grinning and staring.

Slappy's eyes weren't following me as I paced — were they?

I felt a chill run down my back.

It really seemed as if the eyes were watching me, moving as I moved.

I darted to the chair and turned Slappy so that his back was to me. I didn't have time to think about a stupid dummy. My parents would be home from work any minute. And I needed a good story to explain my awful report card.

Did I come up with one? No.

Were my parents upset? Yes.

Mom said she would help me get better organized. Dad said he would help me understand my math problems. The last time Dad helped me with my math, I nearly flunked!

Even Jed — the total goof-off — got a better report card than me. They don't give grades in the lower school. The teacher just writes a report about you.

And Jed's report said that he was a great kid and a really good student. That teacher must be *sick*!

I stared at Jed across the dinner table. He opened his mouth wide to show me a mouth full of chewed-up peas.

Sick!

"You reek," he said to me. For no reason at all.

Sometimes I wonder why families were invented.

Saturday morning, I called Margo. "I can't come over," I told her with a sigh. "My parents won't let me."

"My report card wasn't too good, either," Margo replied. "Miss Carson wrote a note at the bottom. She said I talk too much in class."

"Miss Carson talks too much," I said bitterly.

As I chatted with Margo, I stared at myself in the dresser mirror. *I look too much like Sara,* I thought. *Why do I have to look like her twin? Maybe I'll cut my hair really short. Or get a tattoo.*

I wasn't thinking too clearly.

I was too angry that my parents weren't allowing me to go over to Margo's house.

"This is bad news," Margo said. "I wanted to talk to you about performing with Slappy at my dad's place."

"I know," I replied sadly. "But they're not letting me go anywhere until my science project is finished."

"You still haven't turned that in?" Margo demanded.

"I kind of forgot about it," I confessed. "I did the project part — for the second time. I just have to write the report."

"Well, I told you, Daddy has a birthday party

for a dozen three-year-olds next Saturday," Margo said. "And he wants you and Slappy to entertain them."

"As soon as I finish the science report, I'm going to start rehearsing," I promised. "Tell your dad not to worry, Margo. Tell him I'll be great."

We chatted for a few more minutes. Then my mom shouted for me to get off the phone. I talked for a little while longer — until Mom shouted a second time. Then I said good-bye to Margo and hung up.

I slaved over my computer all morning and most of the afternoon. And I finished the science report.

It wasn't easy. Jed kept coming into my room, begging me to play video games with him. "Just one!" And I had to keep tossing him out.

When I finally finished writing the paper, I printed it out and read it one more time. I thought it was pretty good.

What it needs is a really great-looking cover, I decided.

I wanted to get a bunch of colored markers and do a really bright cover. But my markers were all dried up.

I tossed them into the trash and made my way to Sara's room. I knew that she had an entire drawer filled with colored markers.

Sara was at the mall with a bunch of her

47

friends. Miss Perfect could go out and spend Saturday doing whatever she wanted. Because she was perfect.

I knew she wouldn't mind if I borrowed a few markers.

Jed stopped me outside her door. "One game!" he pleaded. "Just one game!"

"No way," I told him. I placed my hand on top of his head. His red, curly hair felt so soft. I pushed him out of my way. "You always murder me when we play. And I'm not finished with my work yet."

"Why are you going in Sara's room?" he demanded.

"None of your business," I told him.

"You reek," he said. "You double reek, Amy."

I ignored him and made my way into Sara's room to borrow the markers.

I spent nearly an hour making the cover. I filled it with molecules and atoms, all in different colors. *Miss Carson will be impressed,* I decided.

Sara returned home just as I finished. She was carrying a big shopping bag filled with clothes she'd bought at Banana Republic.

She started to her room with the bag. "Mom — come see what I bought," she called.

Mom appeared, carrying a stack of freshly laundered towels.

"Can I see, too?" I called. I followed them to Sara's room.

But Sara stopped at her door.

The bag fell from her hand.

And she let out a scream.

Mom and I crowded behind her. We peered into the bedroom.

What a mess!

Someone had overturned about a dozen jars of paint. Reds, yellows, blues. The paint had spread over Sara's white carpet, like a big, colorful mud puddle.

I gasped and blinked several times. It was unreal!

"I don't believe it!" Sara kept shrieking. "I don't believe it!"

"The carpet is ruined!" Mom exclaimed, taking one step into the room.

The emptied paint jars were on their sides, strewn around the room.

"Jed!" Mom shouted angrily. "Jed — get in here! Now!"

We turned to see Jed right behind us in the hall. "You don't have to shout," he said softly.

Mom narrowed her eyes angrily at my brother. "Jed — how *could* you?" she demanded through clenched teeth.

"Excuse me?" He gazed up at her innocently.

"Jed — don't lie!" Sara screamed. "Did you do this? Did you go in my room again?"

"No way!" Jed protested, shaking his head. "I didn't go in your room today, Sara. Not once.

But I saw Amy go in. And she wouldn't tell me why."

Sara and Mom both turned accusing eyes on me.

"How could you?" Sara screamed, walking around the big paint puddle. "How *could* you?"

"Whoa! Wait! I didn't! I didn't!" I cried frantically.

"I asked Amy why she was going in here," Jed chimed in. "And she said it was none of my business."

"Amy!" Mom cried. "I'm horrified. I'm truly horrified. This — this is *sick*!"

"Yes, it's sick," Sara repeated, shaking her head. "All of my poster paint. All of it. What a mess. I know why you did it. It's because you're jealous of my perfect report card."

"But I didn't do it!" I wailed. "I didn't! I didn't! I didn't!"

"Amy — no one else could have," Mom replied. "If Jed didn't do it, then —"

"But I only came in here to borrow markers!" I cried in a trembling voice. "That's all. I needed markers."

"Amy —" Mom started, pointing to the huge paint puddle.

"I'll show you!" I cried. "I'll show you what I borrowed."

I ran to my room. My hands were shaking as I scooped Sara's markers off my desk. My heart pounded.

How could they accuse me of something so terrible? I asked myself.

Is that what everyone thinks of me? That I'm such a monster?

That I'm so jealous of my sister, I'd pour out all her paints and ruin her rug?

Do they really think I'm crazy?

I ran back to Sara's room, carrying the markers in both hands. Jed sat on Sara's bed, staring down at the thick red, blue, and yellow puddle.

Mom and Sara stood over it, gazing down and shaking their heads. Mom kept making clucking noises with her tongue. She kept pressing her hands against her cheeks.

"Here! See?" I cried. I shoved the markers toward them. "That's why I came in here. I'm not lying!"

Some of the markers fell out of my hands. I bent to pick them up.

"Amy, there were only three of us home this afternoon," Mom said. She was trying to keep her voice low and calm. But she spoke through gritted teeth. "You, me, and Jed."

"I know —" I started.

Mom raised a hand to silence me. "I certainly didn't do this horrible thing," Mom continued. "And Jed says that he didn't do it. So . . ." Her voice trailed off.

"Mom — I'm not a sicko!" I shrieked. "I'm not!"

"You'll feel better if you confess," Mom said. "Then we can talk about this calmly, and —"

"But I didn't do it!" I raged.

With a cry of anger, I flung the markers to the floor. Then I spun around, bolted from Sara's room, and ran down the long hall to my room.

I slammed the door and threw myself face-down onto my bed. I started sobbing loudly. I don't know how long I cried.

Finally, I stood up. My face was sopping wet, and my nose was running. I started to the dresser to get a tissue.

But something caught my eye.

Hadn't I turned Slappy around so that his back was turned to me?

Now he was sitting facing me, staring up at me, his red-lipped grin wider than ever.

Did I turn him back around? Did I?

I didn't remember.

And what did I see on Slappy's shoes?

I wiped the tears from my eyes with the backs of my hands. Then I took a few steps toward the dummy, squinting hard at his big leather shoes.

What *was* that on his shoes?

Red and blue and yellow . . . paint?

Yes.

With a startled gasp, I grabbed both shoes by the heels and raised them close to my face.

Yes.

Drips of paint on Slappy's shoes.

"Slappy — what is going on here?" I asked out loud. "What is going on?"

When Dad came home and saw Sara's room, he nearly exploded.

I was actually worried about him. His face turned as red as a tomato. His chest started heaving in and out. And horrible gurgling noises came up from his throat.

The whole family gathered in the living room. We took our Sharing Night places. Only, this wasn't Family Sharing Night. This was What Are We Going To Do About Amy Night.

"Amy, first you have to tell us the truth," Mom said. She sat stiffly on the couch, squeezing her hands together in her lap.

Dad sat on the other end of the couch, tapping one hand nervously against the couch arm, chewing his lower lip. Jed and Sara sat on the floor against the wall.

"I *am* telling the truth," I insisted shrilly. I slumped in the armchair across from them. My hair fell over my forehead, but I didn't bother to brush it back. My white T-shirt had tearstains on the front, still damp. "If you would only listen to me," I pleaded.

"Okay, we're listening," Mom replied.

"When I went into my room," I started, "there were splashes of paint on Slappy's shoes. And —"

"Enough!" Dad cried, jumping to his feet.

"But, Dad —" I protested.

"Enough!" he insisted. He pointed a finger at me. "No more wild stories, young lady. Storytime is over. We don't want to hear about paint stains on Slappy. We want an explanation for the crime that was committed in Sara's room today."

"But I *am* giving an explanation!" I wailed. "Why did Slappy have paint on his shoes? Why?"

Dad dropped back onto the couch with a sigh. He whispered something to Mom. She whispered back.

I thought I heard them mention the word "doctor."

"Are you — are you going to take me to a psychiatrist?" I asked timidly.

"Do you think you need one?" Mom replied, staring hard at me.

I shook my head. "No."

"Your father and I will talk about this," Mom said. "We will figure out the best thing to do."

The best thing to do?

They grounded me for two weeks. No movies. No friends over. No trips to the mall. No trips anywhere.

I heard them talking about finding me a counselor. But they didn't say anything about it to me.

All week, I could feel them watching me. Studying me as if I were some kind of alien creature.

Sara was pretty cold to me. Her room had to be emptied out and a new rug installed. She wasn't happy about it.

Even Jed treated me differently. He kind of tiptoed around me and kept his distance, as if I had a bad cold or something. He didn't tease me, or tell me that I reek, or call me names.

I really missed it. No kidding.

How did I feel? I felt miserable.

I wanted to get sick. I wanted to catch a really bad stomach flu or something so they'd all feel sorry for me and stop treating me like a criminal.

One good thing: They said I could perform with Slappy at The Party House on Saturday.

Whenever I picked Slappy up, I felt a little weird. I remembered the paint on his shoes and the mess in my sister's room.

But I couldn't come up with one single explanation. So I practiced with Slappy every night.

I had put a lot of good jokes together. Silly jokes I thought little three-year-olds would find funny.

And I studied myself in the mirror. I was getting better at not moving my lips. And it was getting easier to make Slappy's mouth and eyes move correctly.

"Knock knock," I made Slappy say.

"Who's there?" I asked.

"Eddie."

"Eddie who?" I asked.

"Eddie-body got a tissue? I hab a teddible cold!"

And then I pulled back Slappy's head, opened his mouth really wide, and jerked his whole body as I made him sneeze and sneeze and sneeze.

I thought that would really crack up the three-year-olds.

Every night, I worked and worked on our comedy act. I worked so hard.

I didn't know that the act would never go on.

On Saturday afternoon, Mom dropped me off at The Party House. "Have a good show!" she called as she drove away.

I carried Slappy carefully in my arms. Margo met me at the door. She greeted me with an excited smile.

"Just in time!" she cried. "The kids are almost all here. They're total animals!"

"Oh, great!" I muttered, rolling my eyes.

"They're total animals, but they're so cute!" Margo added.

She led me through the twisting hallway to the party room in back. Clusters of red and yellow balloons covered the ceiling. I saw a brightly decorated table, all yellow and red. A balloon on a string floated up from each chair around the table. Each balloon had the name of a guest on it.

The kids really were cute. They were dressed mostly in jeans and bright T-shirts. Two of the girls wore frilly party dresses.

I counted ten of them, all running wildly, chasing each other in the huge room.

Their mothers were grouped around a long table against the back wall. Some of them were sitting down. Some were standing, huddled together, chatting. Some were calling to their kids to stop being so wild.

"I'm helping out, pouring the punch and stuff," Margo told me. "Dad wants you to do your act first thing. You know. To quiet the kids down."

I swallowed hard. "First thing, huh?"

I had been excited. I could barely choke down my tuna fish sandwich at lunch. But now I began to feel nervous. I had major fluttering in my stomach.

Margo led me to the front of the room. I saw a low wooden platform there, painted bright blue. That was the stage.

Seeing the stage made my heart start to pound. My mouth suddenly felt very dry.

Could I really step up on that stage and do my act in front of all these people? Kids and mothers?

I had forgotten that the mothers would all be there. Seeing adults in the audience made me even more nervous.

"Here is the birthday girl," a woman's voice said.

I turned to see a smiling mother. She held the hand of a beautiful little girl. The girl gazed up at me with sparkling blue eyes. She had straight black hair, a lot like mine, only silkier and finer. She had a bright yellow ribbon in her hair. It matched her short yellow party dress and yellow sneakers.

"This is Alicia," the mother announced.

"Hi. I'm Amy," I replied.

"Alicia would like to meet your dummy," the woman said.

"Is he real?" Alicia asked.

I didn't know how to answer that question. "He's a real dummy," I told Alicia.

I propped Slappy up in my arms and slipped my hand into his back. "This is Slappy," I told the little girl. "Slappy, this is Alicia."

"How do you do?" I made Slappy say.

Alicia and her mother both laughed. Alicia stared up at the dummy with her sparkling blue eyes.

"How old are you?" I made Slappy say.

Alicia held up three fingers. "I'm ffffree," she told him.

"Would you like to shake hands with Slappy?" I asked.

Alicia nodded.

I lowered the dummy a little. I pushed forward Slappy's right hand. "Go ahead," I urged Alicia. "Take his hand."

Alicia reached up and grabbed Slappy's hand. She giggled.

"Happy Birthday," Slappy said.

Alicia shook his hand gently. Then she started to back away.

"We can't wait to see your show," Alicia's mother said to me. "I know the kids are going to love it."

"I hope so!" I replied. My stomach fluttered again. I was still really nervous.

"Let go!" Alicia cried. She tugged at Slappy's hand. She giggled. "He won't let go!"

Alicia's mom laughed. "What a funny dummy!" She grabbed Alicia's other hand. "Let go of the dummy, honey. We have to get everyone in their seats for the show."

Alicia tugged a little harder. "But he won't let go of *me*, Mommy!" she cried. "He wants to shake hands!"

Alicia gave a hard tug. But her tiny hand was still wrapped up inside Slappy's. She giggled. "He likes me. He won't let go."

"Oh, look," her mother said, glancing to the door. "Phoebe and Jennifer just arrived. Let's go say hi."

Alicia tried to follow her mom, but Slappy held tight to her hand. Alicia's smile faded. "Let *go!*" she insisted.

I saw that several kids had gathered around. They watched Alicia tug at Slappy's hand.

"Let go! Let me go!" Alicia cried angrily.

I leaned over to examine Slappy's hand. To my surprise, it appeared that his hand had clenched tightly around hers.

Alicia gave a hard tug. "Ow! He's hurting me, Mommy!"

More kids came over to watch. Some of them were laughing. Two little dark-haired boys exchanged frightened glances.

"Please — make him let go!" Alicia wailed. She tugged again and again.

I froze in panic. My mind whirred. I tried to think of what to do.

Had Alicia gotten her hand caught somehow?

Slappy's hand couldn't really close around hers — could it?

Alicia's mother was staring at me angrily. "Please let Alicia's hand out," she said impatiently.

"He's hurting me!" Alicia cried. "Ow! He's squeezing my hand!"

The room grew very quiet. The other kids

were all watching now. Their eyes wide. Their expressions confused.

I didn't know what to do. I had no control for Slappy's hands.

My heart pounded in my chest. I tried to make a joke of it. "Slappy really likes you!" I told Alicia.

But the little girl was sobbing now. Little tears rolled down her cheeks. "Mommy — make him stop!"

I pulled my hand out from Slappy's back. I grabbed his wooden hand between my hands. "Let go of her, Slappy!" I demanded.

I tried pulling the fingers open.

But I couldn't budge them.

"What is wrong?" Alicia's mother was screaming. "Is her hand caught? What are you doing to her?"

"He's hurting me!" Alicia wailed. "Owwww! He's squeezing me!"

Several kids were crying now. Mothers rushed across the room to comfort them.

Alicia's sobs rose up over the frightened cries of the other three-year-olds. The harder she tugged, the tighter the wooden hand squeezed.

"Let go, Slappy!" I shrieked, pulling his fingers. "Let go! Let go!"

"I don't understand!" Alicia's mother cried. She began frantically tugging my arm. "What are you doing? Let her go! Let her go!"

"Owwwww!" Alicia uttered a high, heart-

63

breaking wail. "Make him stop! It hurts! It hurts!"

And then Slappy suddenly tilted his head back. His eyes opened wide, and his mouth opened in a long, evil laugh.

I burst into the house and let the screen door
slam behind me. I had taken the city bus to
Logan Street. Then I had run the six blocks to
my house with Slappy hanging over my
shoulder.

"Amy, how did it go?" Mom called from the
kitchen. "Did you get a ride? I thought we were
supposed to come pick you up."

I didn't answer her. I was sobbing too hard.
I ran down the hall to my room and slammed
the door.

I hoisted Slappy off my shoulder and tossed
him into the closet. I never wanted to see him
again. Never.

I caught a glimpse of myself in the dresser
mirror. My cheeks were swollen and puffy from
crying. My eyes were red. My hair was wet and
tangled and matted to my forehead.

I took several deep breaths and tried to stop
crying.

I kept hearing that poor little girl's screams

in my ears. Slappy finally let go of her after he uttered his ugly laugh.

But Alicia couldn't stop crying. She was so frightened! And her little hand was red and swollen.

The other kids were all screaming and crying, too.

Alicia's mother was furious. She called Margo's dad out from the kitchen. She was shaking and sputtering with anger. She said she was going to sue The Party House.

Margo's dad quietly asked me to leave. He led me to the front door. He said it wasn't my fault. But he said the kids were too frightened of Slappy now. There was no way I could do my show.

I saw Margo hurrying over to me. But I turned and ran out the door.

I had never been so upset. I didn't know what to do. A light rain had started to come down. I watched rainwater flow down the curb and into the sewer drain. I wanted to flow away with it.

Now I threw myself onto my bed.

I kept picturing little Alicia, screaming and crying, trying to twist out of Slappy's grasp.

Mom knocked hard on my bedroom door. "Amy? Amy — what are you doing? What's wrong?"

"Go away!" I wailed. "Just go away."

But she opened the door and stepped into the room. Sara came in behind her, a confused

66

expression on her face.

"Amy — the show didn't go well?" Mom asked softly.

"Go away!" I sobbed. "Please!"

"Amy, you'll do better next time," Sara said, stepping up to the bed. She put a hand on my trembling shoulder.

"Shut up!" I cried. "Shut up, Miss Perfect!"

I didn't mean to sound so angry. I was out of control.

Sara stepped back, hurt.

"Tell us what happened," Mom insisted. "You'll feel better if you tell us."

I pulled myself up until I was sitting on the edge of the bed. I wiped my eyes and brushed my wet hair off my face.

And then, suddenly, the whole story burst out of me.

I told how Slappy grabbed Alicia's hand and wouldn't let go. And how all the kids were crying. And the parents were all screaming and making a fuss. And how I had to leave without doing my act.

And then I leaped to my feet, threw my arms around my mom, and started to sob again.

She petted my hair, the way she used to do when I was a little girl. She kept whispering, "Ssshh shhhh shhhh."

Slowly, I began to calm down.

"This is so weird," Sara murmured, shaking her head.

"I'm a little worried about you," Mom said, holding my hands. "The little girl got her hand caught. That's all. You don't really believe that the dummy grabbed her hand — do you?"

Mom stared at me hard, studying me.

She thinks I'm crazy, I realized. *She thinks I'm totally messed up.*

She doesn't believe me.

I decided I'd better not insist that my story was true. I shook my head. "Yeah. I guess her hand got caught," I said, lowering my eyes to the floor.

"Maybe you should put Slappy away for a while," Mom suggested, biting her bottom lip.

"Yeah. You're right," I agreed. I pointed. "I already put him in the closet."

"Good idea," Mom replied. "Leave him in there for a while. I think you've been spending too much time with that dummy."

"Yeah. You need a new hobby," Sara chimed in.

"It wasn't a hobby!" I snapped.

"Well, leave him in the closet for a few days — okay, Amy?" Mom said.

I nodded. "I never want to see him again," I muttered.

I thought I heard a sigh from inside the closet. But, of course, that was my imagination.

"Get yourself cleaned up," Mom instructed. "Wash your face. Then come to the kitchen and I'll make you a snack."

"Okay," I agreed.

Sara followed Mom out the door. "Weird," I heard Sara mutter. "Amy is getting so weird."

Margo called after dinner. She said she felt terrible about what had happened. She said her dad didn't blame me. "He wants to give you another chance," Margo told me. "Maybe with older kids."

"Thanks," I replied. "But I put Slappy away for a while. I don't know if I want to be a ventriloquist anymore."

"At the party today — what happened?" Margo asked. "What went wrong?"

"I don't really know," I said. "I don't really know."

That night, I went to bed early. Before I turned out the light, I glanced at the closet door. It was closed tightly.

Having Slappy shut up in the closet made me feel safer.

I fell asleep quickly. I slept a deep, dreamless sleep.

When I awoke the next morning, I sat up and rubbed my eyes.

Then I heard Sara's angry screams down the hall.

"Mom! Dad! Mom! Hurry!" Sara was shouting. "Come see what Amy did now!"

69

I shut my eyes, listening to my sister's screams.

What now? I thought with a shudder. *What now?*

"Ohh!" I let out a low cry when I saw that my closet door was open a crack.

My heart pounding, I climbed out of bed and began running down the hall to Sara's room. Mom, Dad, and Jed were already on their way.

"Mom! Dad! Look what she did!" Sara screamed.

"Oh, no!" I heard Mom and Dad shriek.

I stopped in the doorway, peered in — and gasped.

Sara's bedroom walls! They were smeared with red paint!

Someone had taken a thick paintbrush and had scrawled *AMY AMY AMY AMY* in huge red letters all over Sara's walls.

"Noooo!" I moaned. I covered my mouth with both hands to stop the sound.

My eyes darted from wall to wall, reading my

name over and over.

AMY AMY AMY AMY.

Why *my* name?

I suddenly felt sick. I swallowed hard, trying to force back my nausea.

I blinked several times, trying to blink the ugly red scrawls away.

AMY AMY AMY AMY.

"Why?" Sara asked me in a trembling voice. She adjusted her nightshirt and leaned against her dresser. "Why, Amy?"

I suddenly realized that everyone was staring at me.

"I — I — I —" I sputtered.

"Amy, this cannot continue," Dad said solemnly. His expression wasn't angry. It was sad.

"We'll get you some help, dear," Mom said. She had tears in her eyes. Her chin trembled.

Jed stood silently with his arms crossed in front of his pajama shirt.

"Why, Amy?" Sara demanded again.

"But — I *didn't*!" I finally choked out.

"Amy — no stories," Mom said softly.

"But, Mom — I didn't do it!" I insisted shrilly.

"This is serious," Dad murmured, rubbing his whiskery chin. "Amy, do you realize how serious this is?"

Jed reached out two fingers and rubbed them over one of the red paint scrawls. "Dry," he reported.

"That means it was done early in the night,"

Dad said, his eyes locked on me. "Do you realize how bad this is? This isn't just mischief."

I took a deep breath. My whole body was shaking. "Slappy did it!" I blurted out. "I'm not crazy, Dad! I'm not! You've got to believe me! Slappy did it!"

"Amy, please —" Mom said softly.

"Come with me!" I cried. "I'll prove it. I'll prove that Slappy did it. Come on!"

I didn't wait for them to reply. I turned and bolted from the room.

I flew down the hall. They all followed silently behind me.

"Is Amy sick or something?" I heard Jed ask my parents.

I didn't hear the answer.

I burst into my room. They hurried close behind.

I stepped up to the closet and pulled the door open.

"See?" I cried, pointing to Slappy. "See? That proves it! Slappy did it!"

I pointed triumphantly at Slappy. "See? See?"

The dummy sat crossed-legged on the closet floor. His head stood erect on his narrow shoulders. He appeared to grin up at us.

Slappy's left hand rested on the closet floor. His right hand was in his lap.

And in his right hand he clutched a fat paintbrush.

The bristles on the brush were caked with red paint.

"I *told* you Slappy did it!" I cried, stepping back so the others could get a better view.

But everyone remained silent. Mom and Dad frowned and shook their heads.

Jed's giggle broke the silence. "This is dumb," he told Sara.

Sara lowered her eyes and didn't reply.

"Oh, Amy," Mom said, sighing. "Did you really think you could blame it on the dummy by putting the paintbrush in his hand?"

"Huh?" I cried. I didn't understand what

Mom was saying.

"Did you really expect us to believe this?" Dad asked softly. His eyes stared hard into mine.

"Did you think you could put the brush into Slappy's hand, and make us think he painted your name on Sara's walls?"

"But I *didn't*!" I shrieked.

"When did he learn how to spell?" Jed chimed in.

"Be quiet, Jed," Dad said sharply. "This is serious. It isn't a joke."

"Sara, take Jed out of here," Mom instructed. "The two of you go to the kitchen and get breakfast started."

Sara began to guide Jed to the door. But he pulled away. "I want to stay!" he cried. "I want to see how you punish Amy."

"Get!" Mom cried, shooing him away with both hands.

Sara tugged him out of the room.

I was shaking all over. I narrowed my eyes at Slappy. Had his grin grown even wider?

I stared at the paintbrush in his hand. The red paint on the bristles blurred, blurred until I saw only red.

I blinked several times and turned back to my parents. "You really don't believe me?" I asked softly, my voice trembling.

They shook their heads. "How can we believe you, dear?" Mom replied.

"We can't believe that a wooden dummy has been doing these horrible things in Sara's room," Dad added. "Why don't you tell us the truth, Amy?"

"But I *am*!" I protested.

How could I prove it to them? How?

I let out an angry cry and slammed the closet door shut.

"Let's try to calm down," Mom urged quietly. "Let's all get dressed and have some breakfast. We can talk about this when we're feeling better."

"Good idea," Dad replied, still squinting at me through his glasses. He was studying me as if he'd never seen me before.

He scratched his bald head. "Guess I'll have to call a painter for Sara's room. It'll take at least two coats to cover up the red."

They turned and made their way slowly from my room, talking about how much it was going to cost to have my sister's room painted.

I stood in the center of the room and shut my eyes. Every time I closed them, I saw red. All over Sara's wall:

AMY AMY AMY AMY.

"But I didn't do it!" I cried out loud.

My heart pounding, I spun around. I grabbed the knob and jerked open the closet door.

I grabbed Slappy by the shoulders of his gray jacket and pulled him up from the floor.

The paintbrush fell from his hand. It landed

with a thud beside my bare foot.

I shook the dummy angrily. Shook him so hard that his arms and legs swung back and forth, and his head snapped back.

Then I lifted him so that we were eye to eye.

"Admit it!" I screamed, glaring into his grinning face. "Go ahead! Admit that you did it! Tell me that you did it!"

The glassy blue eyes gazed up at me.

Lifelessly.

Blankly.

Neither of us moved.

And then, to my horror, the wooden lips parted. The red mouth slowly opened.

And Slappy let out a soft, evil, *"Hee hee hee."*

"I can't come over," I told Margo glumly. I was sprawled on top of my bed, the phone pressed against my ear. "I'm not allowed out of my room all day."

"Huh? Why?" Margo demanded.

I sighed. "If I told you, Margo, you wouldn't believe me."

"Try me," she replied.

I decided not to tell her. I mean, my whole family thought I was crazy. Why should my best friend think it, too?

"Maybe I'll tell you about it when I see you," I said.

Silence at the other end.

Then Margo uttered, "Wow."

"Wow? What does *wow* mean?" I cried.

"Wow. It must be pretty bad if you can't talk about it, Amy."

"It — it's just weird," I stammered. "Can we change the subject?"

Another silence. "Daddy has a birthday party

for six-year-olds coming up, Amy. And he wondered —"

"No. Sorry," I broke in quickly. "I put Slappy away."

"Excuse me?" Margo reacted with surprise.

"I put the dummy away," I told her. "I'm finished with that. I'm not going to be a ventriloquist anymore."

"But, Amy —" Margo protested. "You *loved* playing with those dummies. And you said you wanted to make some money, remember? So Daddy —"

"No," I repeated firmly. "I changed my mind, Margo. I'm sorry. Tell your dad I'm sorry. I — I'll tell you about it when I see you."

I swallowed hard. And added: "*If* I ever see you."

"You sound terrible," Margo replied softly. "Should I come over to your house? I think I could get my dad to drop me off."

"I'm totally grounded," I said unhappily. "No visitors."

I heard footsteps in the hall. Probably Mom or Dad checking up on me. I wasn't allowed to be on the phone, either.

"Got to go. Bye, Margo," I whispered. I hung up the phone.

Mom knocked on my bedroom door. I recognized her knock. "Amy, want to talk?" she called in.

"Not really," I replied glumly.

"As soon as you tell the truth, you can come out," Mom said.

"I know," I muttered.

"Why don't you just tell the truth now? It's such a beautiful day," Mom called in. "Don't waste the whole day in your room."

"I — I don't feel like talking now," I told her.

She didn't say anything else. But I could hear her standing out there. Finally I heard her footsteps padding back down the hall.

I grabbed my pillow and buried my face in it.

I wanted to shut out the world. And think.

Think. Think. Think.

I wasn't going to confess to a crime I didn't do. No way.

I was going to find a way to prove to them that Slappy was the culprit. And I was going to prove to them that I wasn't crazy.

I had to show them that Slappy wasn't an ordinary dummy.

He was alive. And he was evil.

But how could I prove it?

I climbed to my feet and began pacing back and forth. I stopped at the window and gazed out at the front yard.

It *was* a beautiful spring day. Bright yellow tulips bobbed in the flower patch in front of my window. The sky was a solid blue. The twin maple trees in the center of the yard were starting to unfurl fresh leaves.

I took a deep breath. The air smelled so fresh

and sweet.

I saw Jed and a couple of his friends. They were skating down the sidewalk. Laughing. Having a good time.

And I was a prisoner. A prisoner in my room.

All because of Slappy.

I spun away from the window and stared at the closet door. I had shoved Slappy into the back of the closet and shut the door tightly.

I'm going to catch you in the act, Slappy, I decided.

That's how I'm going to prove I'm not crazy.

I'm going to stay up all night. I'm going to stay up every night. And the first time you creep out of that closet, I'll be awake. And I'll follow you.

And I'll make sure that everyone sees what you are doing.

I'll make sure that everyone sees that you are the evil one in this house.

I felt so upset. I knew I wasn't really thinking clearly.

But having a plan made me feel a little better.

Taking one last glance at the closet door, I crossed the room to my desk and started to do my homework.

Mom and Dad let me come out for dinner.

Dad had grilled hamburgers in the backyard, the first barbecue of spring. I loved grilled hamburgers, especially when they're charred real black. But I could barely taste my food.

I guess I felt too excited and nervous about trapping Slappy.

No one talked much.

Mom kept chattering to Dad about the vegetable garden and what she wanted to plant. Sara talked a little about the mural she had started to paint in her room. Jed kept complaining about how he wrecked his knee skating.

No one spoke to me. They kept glancing over the table at me. Studying me like I was some kind of zoo animal.

I asked to be excused before dessert.

I usually stay up till ten. But a little after nine, I decided to go to bed.

I was wide awake. Eager to trap Slappy.

I turned out the light and tucked myself in. Then I lay staring up at the shifting shadows on the bedroom ceiling, waiting, waiting . . .

Waiting for Slappy to come creeping out of the closet.

I must have fallen asleep.

I tried not to. But I must have drifted off anyway.

I was startled awake by sounds in the room.

I raised my head, instantly alert. And listened.

The scrape of feet on my carpet. A soft rustling.

A shiver of fear ran down my back. I felt

goosebumps up and down my arms.

Another low sound. So near my bed.

I reached forward quickly. Clicked on the bed table lamp.

And cried out.

"Jed — what are you *doing* in here?" I shrieked.

He stood blinking at me in the center of the room. One leg of his blue pajama pants had rolled up. His red hair was matted against one side of his head.

"What are you doing in my room?" I demanded breathlessly.

He squinted at me. "Huh? Why are you yelling at me? You *called* me, Amy."

"I — I *what*?" I sputtered.

"You called me. I heard you." He rubbed his eyes with his fingers and yawned. "I was asleep. You woke me up."

I lowered my feet to the floor and stood up. My legs felt shaky and weak. Jed had really scared me.

"I was asleep, too," I told him. "I didn't call you."

"Yes, you did," he insisted. "You told me to come to your room." He bent to pull down the pajama leg.

"Jed, you just woke *me* up," I replied. "So how could I call you?"

He scratched his hair. He yawned again. "You mean I dreamed it?"

I studied his face. "Jed — did you sneak into my room to play some kind of prank?" I demanded sternly.

He wrinkled his face up, tried to appear innocent.

"*Did* you?" I demanded. "Were you going into the closet to do something with Slappy?"

"No way!" he protested. He started to back out of the room. "I'm telling the truth, Amy. I thought you called me. That's all."

I squinted hard at him, trying to decide if he was telling the truth. I let my eyes wander around the room. Everything seemed okay. Dennis lay in the armchair, his head in his lap.

The closet door remained closed.

"It was a dream, that's all," Jed repeated. "Good night, Amy."

I said good night. "Sorry I got upset, Jed. It's been a bad day."

I listened to him pad back to his room.

The cat poked his head into my room, his eyes gleaming like gold. "Go to sleep, George," I whispered. "You go to sleep, too, okay?" He obediently turned and disappeared.

I clicked off the bed table lamp and settled back into bed.

Jed was telling the truth, I decided. He

84

seemed as confused as I was.

My eyes suddenly felt heavy. As if there were hundred-pound weights over them. I let out a loud yawn.

I felt so sleepy. And the pillow felt so soft and warm.

But I couldn't let myself fall back to sleep.

I had to stay awake. Had to wait for Slappy to make his move.

Did I drift back to sleep? I'm not sure.

A loud *click* made my eyes shoot open wide.

I raised my head in time to see the closet door start to open.

The room lay in darkness. No light washed in from the window. The door was a black shadow, sliding slowly, slowly.

My heart began to pound. My mouth suddenly felt dry as cotton.

The closet door slid slowly, silently.

A low *creak*.

And then a shadow stepped out from behind the dark door.

I squinted hard at it. Not moving a muscle.

Another *creak* of the door.

The figure took another silent step. Out of the closet. Another step. Another. Making its way past my bed, to the bedroom door.

Slappy.

Yes!

Even in the night blackness I could see his large, rounded head. I watched his skinny arms dangle at his sides, the wooden hands bobbing as he moved.

The heavy leather shoes slid over my carpet. The thin, boneless legs nearly collapsed with each shuffling step.

Like a scarecrow, I thought, gripped with horror.

He walks like a scarecrow. Because he has no bones. No bones at all.

Up and down, his whole body bobbed as he crept away.

I waited until he slithered and scraped out the door and into the hall. Then I jumped to my feet.

I took a deep breath and held it.

Then I tiptoed through the darkness after him.

Here we go! I told myself. *Here we go!*

I stopped at the bedroom door and poked my head into the hall. Mom keeps a small night-light on all night just outside her bedroom door. It cast dim yellow light over the other end of the hall.

Peering into the light, I watched Slappy pull himself silently toward Sara's room. The big shoes shuffled along the carpet. Slappy's body bobbed and bent. The big wooden hands nearly dragged along the floor.

When my chest started to ache, I realized I hadn't taken a breath. As silently as I could, I let out a long whoosh of air. Then I took another deep breath and started to follow Slappy down the hall.

I had a sudden impulse to shout: "Mom! Dad!"

They would burst out of their room and see Slappy standing there in the middle of the hall.

But, no.

I didn't want to shout for them now. I wanted to see where Slappy was heading. I wanted to see what he planned to do.

I took a step. The floorboard creaked under my bare foot.

Did he hear me?

I pressed my back against the wall, tried to squeeze myself flat in the deep shadows.

I peered through the dim yellow light at him. He kept bobbing silently along. His shoulders rode up and down with each shuffling step.

He was just outside Sara's room when he turned around.

My heart stopped.

I ducked low. Dropped back into the bathroom.

Had he seen me?

Had he turned around because he knew I was there?

I shut my eyes. Waited. Listened.

Listened for him to come scraping back. Listened for him to turn around and come back to get me.

Silence.

I swallowed hard. My mouth felt so dry. My legs were trembling. I grabbed the tile wall to steady myself.

Still silent out there.

I gathered up my courage and slowly, slowly poked my head out into the hall.

Empty.

I squinted toward Sara's room in the yellow light.

No one there.

He's in Sara's room, I told myself. *He's doing something terrible in Sara's room. Something I'll be blamed for.*

Not this *time, Slappy!* I silently vowed.

This time you're going to be caught.

Pressing against the wall, I crept down the hall.

I stopped in Sara's doorway.

The night-light was plugged in across from Sara's room. The light was brighter here.

I squinted into her bedroom. I could see the mural she had started to paint. A beach scene. The ocean. A broad, yellow beach. Kites flying over the beach. Kids building a sand castle in one corner. The mural was tacked up, nearly covering the entire wall.

Where was Slappy?

I took a step into the room — and saw him.

Standing at her paint table.

I saw his big wooden hand fumble over the table of supplies. Then he grabbed a paintbrush in one hand.

He raised and lowered the brush, as if pretending to paint the air.

Then I saw him dip the paintbrush in a jar of paint.

Slappy took a step toward the mural. Then another step.

He stood for a moment, admiring the mural.

He raised the paintbrush high.

That's when I burst into the room.

I dove toward the dummy just as he raised the paintbrush to the mural.

I grabbed the paintbrush with one hand. Wrapped my other hand around his waist. And tugged him back.

The dummy kicked both legs and tried to punch me with his fists.

"Hey!" a startled voice shouted.

The light clicked on.

Slappy went limp on my arm. His head dropped. His arms and legs dangled to the floor.

Sitting up in bed, Sara gaped at me in horror.

I saw her eyes stop at the paintbrush in my hand.

"Amy — what are you *doing*?" she cried.

And, then, without waiting for an answer, Sara began to shout: "Mom! Dad! Hurry! She's in here again!"

Dad came rumbling in first, adjusting his pajama pants. "What's going on? What's the problem?"

Mom followed right behind him, blinking and yawning.

"I — I took this from Slappy," I stammered, holding up the paintbrush. "He — he was going to ruin the mural."

They stared at the paintbrush in my hand.

"I heard Slappy sneak out of the closet," I explained breathlessly. "I followed him into Sara's room. I grabbed him just before — before he did something terrible."

I turned to Sara. "You saw Slappy — right? You saw him?"

"Yeah," Sara said, still in bed, her arms crossed over her chest. "I see Slappy. You're carrying him on your arm."

The dummy hung over my arm, its head nearly hitting the floor.

"No!" I cried to Sara. "You saw him sneak

91

into your room — right? That's why you turned on the light?"

Sara rolled her eyes. "I saw *you* come into my room," she replied. "You're *carrying* the dummy, Amy. You're holding the dummy — and the brush."

"But — but — but —" I sputtered.

My eyes darted from face to face. They all stared back at me as if I had just landed on Earth in a flying saucer.

No one in my family was going to believe me. No one.

The next morning, Mom hung up the phone as I came down for breakfast. "You're wearing shorts to school?" she asked, eyeing my outfit — olive-green shorts and a red sleeveless T-shirt.

"The weatherman said it's going to be hot," I replied.

Jed and Sara were already at the table. They glanced up from their cereal bowls, but didn't say anything.

I poured myself a glass of grape juice. I'm the only one in my family who doesn't like orange juice. I guess I *am* totally weird.

"Who were you talking to on the phone?" I asked Mom. I took a long drink.

"Uh . . . Dr. Palmer's secretary," she replied hesitantly. "You have purple above your lip," she told me, pointing.

I wiped the grape juice off with a napkin. "Dr.

Palmer? Isn't she a shrink?" I asked.

Mom nodded. "I tried to get an appointment for today. But she can't see you until Wednesday."

"But, Mom!" I protested.

Mom placed a finger over her mouth. "Sssshhh. No discussion."

"But, Mom!" I repeated.

"Ssshhh. Just talk to her once, Amy. You might enjoy it. You might think it's helpful."

"Yeah. Sure," I muttered.

I turned to Sara and Jed. They stared down at their cereal bowls.

I sighed and set the juice glass down in the sink.

I knew what this meant. It meant that I had until Wednesday to prove to my family that I wasn't a total wack job.

In the lunchroom at school, Margo begged me to tell her what was going on with me. "Why were you locked up in your room all day yesterday?" she demanded. "Come on, Amy — spill."

"It's no big deal," I lied.

No way I was going to tell her.

I didn't need the story going around school that Amy Kramer believes her ventriloquist dummy is alive.

I didn't need everyone whispering about me and staring at me the way everyone in my family did.

"Dad wants to know if you'll change your

mind about the birthday party," Margo said. "If you want to perform with Slappy, you can —"

"No. Forget it!" I interrupted. "I put Slappy in the closet, and he's staying there. Forever."

Margo's eyes went wide. "Okay. Okay. Wow. You don't have to bite my head off."

"Sorry," I said quickly. "I'm a little stressed out these days. Here. Want this?" I handed her the brownie Mom had packed.

"Thanks," Margo replied, surprised.

"Later," I said. I crinkled up my lunch bag, tossed it in the trash, and hurried away.

In my room that night, I couldn't concentrate on my homework. I kept staring at the calendar.

Monday night. I had only two nights to prove that I wasn't crazy, that Slappy really was doing these horrible things.

I slammed my history book shut. No way I could read about the firing on Fort Sumter tonight.

I paced back and forth for a while. Thinking. Thinking hard. But getting nowhere.

What could I do?

What?

After a while, my head felt about to split open. I reached up both hands and tugged at my hair.

"Aaaaagh!" I let out a furious cry. Of anger. Of frustration.

Maybe I'll just get rid of Slappy, I decided.

Maybe I'll take him outside and toss him in the trash.

And that will end the whole problem.

The idea made me feel a little better.

I turned and took two steps toward the closet.

But I stopped with a gasp when I saw the doorknob slowly turn.

As I stared in shock, the closet door swung open.

Slappy stepped out.

He slumped forward and stopped a few feet in front of me.

His blue eyes glared up at me. His grin grew wider.

"Amy," he rasped, "it's time you and I had a little talk."

"Amy, now you are my slave," Slappy said. His threat came out in a harsh, cold rasp. The eerie voice made me shiver.

I stared back at him. I couldn't reply.

I gaped into those glassy blue eyes, that red-lipped smirk.

"You read the ancient words that bring me to life," the dummy whispered. "And now you will serve me. You will do everything I ask."

"No!" I finally managed to choke out. "No! Please!"

"Yes!" he cried. The grinning wooden head bobbed up and down, nodding. "Yes, Amy! You are my slave now! My slave forever!"

"I w-won't!" I stammered. "You can't make me —" My voice caught in my throat. My legs wobbled like rubber. My knees buckled, and I nearly fell.

Slappy raised one hand and grabbed my wrist. I felt the cold wooden fingers tighten around me. "You will do as I tell you — from now on," the dummy whispered. "Or else . . ."

"Let go of me!" I cried. I struggled to tug my arm free. But his grasp was too tight. "Or else *what*?" I cried.

"Or else I will destroy your sister's mural," Slappy replied. His painted grin grew wider. The cold eyes glared into mine.

"Big deal," I muttered. "Do you really think I'll be your slave because you wreck her painting?
You've already wrecked Sara's room — haven't you? That doesn't mean I'll be your slave!"

"I'll keep on destroying things," Slappy replied, tightening his grip on my wrist, tugging me down toward him. "Maybe I'll start wrecking your brother's things, too. And you will be blamed, Amy. You will be blamed for it all."

"Stop —" I cried, trying to twist free.

"Your parents are already worried about you — aren't they, Amy?" the dummy rasped in that harsh, cold, whispery voice. "Your parents already think you're crazy!"

"Stop! Please!" I pleaded.

"What do you think they'll do when you start wrecking everything in the house?" Slappy demanded. "What do you think they'll do to you, Amy?"

"Listen to me!" I shrieked. "You can't —"

He jerked my arm hard. "They'll send you away!" he rasped, his eyes flashing wildly.

"That's what your parents will do. They'll send you away. And you'll never see them again — except on visiting days!"

He tilted back his wooden head and uttered a shrill laugh.

A low moan escaped my throat. My entire body shuddered with terror.

Slappy tugged me closer. "You will be an excellent slave," he whispered in my ear. "You and I will have many good years together. You will devote your life to me."

"No!" I cried. "No, I won't!"

I sucked in a deep breath. Then I swung my arm hard, as hard as I could.

I caught the dummy by surprise.

Before he could let go of my wrist, I pulled him off balance.

He let out a startled grunt as I lifted him off the floor.

He's just a dummy, I told myself. *Just a dummy. I can handle him. I can beat him.*

His hand fell off my wrist.

I ducked low. Grabbed his boneless arm with both hands. Swung my shoulder. Flipped him over my back.

He landed hard on his stomach. His head made a loud *clonk* as it hit the floor.

Breathing hard, my heart thudding wildly, I dove.

I can handle him. I can beat him.

I tried to pin him to the floor with my knees.

But he spun away and scrambled up, faster than I could believe.

I cried out as he swung his wooden fist.

I tried to dodge away. But he was too fast.

The heavy fist hit me square in the forehead.

My face felt as if it had exploded. Pain shot down my body.

Everything went bright red.

And, holding both sides of my head, I crumpled to the floor.

I can handle him. I can beat him.

The words repeated in my mind.

I blinked my eyes. Raised my head.

I refused to give up.

Through the haze of red, I reached up with both hands.

I grabbed Slappy by the waist and pulled him down.

Ignoring my throbbing forehead, I wrestled him to the ground. He kicked both feet and thrashed his arms wildly. He swung at me, trying to land another blow.

But I dug my knee into his middle. Then I wrapped my hands around his thrashing arms and pinned them to the floor.

"Let go, slave!" he squealed. "I command you — let go!" He struggled and squirmed.

But I held tight.

His eyes darted frantically from side to side. His wooden jaw clicked open and shut, open and shut, as he strained to squirm free.

"I command you to let go, slave! You have no choice! You must obey me!"

I ignored his shrill cries and swung his arms behind his back. Holding them tightly in place, I climbed to my feet.

He tried to kick me with both shoes. But I let go of the arms and grabbed his legs.

I swung him upside down. Once again, his head hit the floor with a *clonk*.

It didn't seem to hurt him a bit.

"Let go! Let go, slave! You will pay! You will pay dearly for this!" He screamed and protested, squirming and swinging his arms.

Breathing hard, I dragged him across the rug — and swung him into the open closet.

He dove quickly, trying to escape.

But I slammed the door in his face. And turned the lock.

With a sigh, I leaned my back against the closet door and struggled to catch my breath.

"Let me out! You can't keep me in here!" Slappy raged.

He began pounding on the door. Then he kicked the door.

"I'll break it down! I really will!" he threatened. He pounded even harder. The big wooden hands thudded against the wooden door.

I turned and saw the door start to give.

He's going to break it open! I realized.

What can I do? What can I do now? I tried to fight back my panic, struggled to think

101

clearly.

Slappy furiously kicked at the door.

I need help, I decided.

I bolted into the hall. Mom and Dad had their bedroom door closed, I saw. *Should I wake them up?*

No. They wouldn't believe me.

I'd drag them into my room. Slappy would be slumped lifelessly on the closet floor. Mom and Dad would be even more upset about me.

Sara, I thought. *Maybe I can convince Sara. Maybe Sara will listen to me.*

Her door was open. I burst into her bedroom.

She stood at the mural, brush in hand, dabbing yellow paint on the beach.

She turned as I ran in, and her face tightened in anger. "Amy — what do *you* want?" she demanded.

"You — you've got to believe me!" I sputtered. "I need your help! It wasn't me who did those horrible things. It really wasn't, Sara. It was Slappy. Please — believe me! It was Slappy!"

"Yes. I know," Sara replied calmly.

21

"Huh?" My mouth dropped open. I stared at her in surprise. "What did you say?"

Sara set down the paintbrush. She wiped her hands on her gray smock. "Amy — I know it's Slappy," she repeated in a whisper.

"I — I —" I was so stunned, I couldn't speak. "But, Sara — you —"

"I'm sorry. I'm so sorry!" she cried with emotion. She rushed forward and threw her arms around me. She hugged me tightly.

I still didn't believe what she had said. My head was spinning.

I gently pushed her away. "You knew all this time? You knew it was Slappy and not me?"

Sara nodded. "The other night, I woke up. I heard someone in my room. I pretended to be asleep. But I had my eyes open partway."

"And?" I demanded.

"I saw Slappy," Sara confessed, lowering her eyes. "I saw him carrying a red paintbrush. I saw him painting *AMY AMY AMY AMY* all over my walls."

"But you didn't tell Mom and Dad?" I cried. "You made them think it was me? And the whole time, you knew the truth?"

Sara kept her eyes on the floor. Her black hair fell over her face. She brushed it back with a quick, nervous sweep of one hand.

"I — I didn't want to believe it," she confessed. "I didn't want to believe that a dummy could walk on its own, that it could be . . . alive."

I glared at her. "And, so?"

"So I accused you," Sara said with a sob. "I guess the truth was just too scary. I was too frightened, Amy. I *wanted* to believe it was you doing those horrible things. I wanted to pretend it wasn't the dummy."

"You *wanted* to get me in trouble," I accused. "That's why you did it, Sara. That's why you lied to Mom and Dad. You *wanted* to get me in trouble."

She finally raised her face to me. I saw two tears trailing down her cheeks. "Yeah, I guess," she murmured.

She wiped the tears off with her hands. Her green eyes locked on mine. "I — I guess I'm a little jealous of you," she said.

"Huh?" My sister had stunned me again. I squinted at her, trying to make sense of her words. "You?" I cried. "You're jealous of *me*?"

She nodded. "Yeah. I guess. Everything is easy for you. You're so relaxed. Everyone likes your sense of humor. It's not like that for me," Sara explained. "I have to paint to impress people."

I opened my mouth, but no sound came out.

This had to be the biggest surprise of all. Sara jealous of *me*?

Didn't she know how jealous I was of *her*?

I suddenly had a funny feeling in my chest. My eyes brimmed with tears. Strong emotion swept over me like an ocean wave.

I rushed forward and hugged Sara.

For some reason, we both started laughing. I can't explain it. We stood there in the middle of her room, laughing like lunatics.

I guess we were just so glad that the truth was out.

Then Slappy's painted face flashed back into my mind. And I remembered with a chill why I had burst into my sister's room.

"You have to help me," I told her. "Right now."

Sara's smile vanished. "Help you do what?" she demanded.

"We have to get rid of Slappy," I told her. "We have to get rid of him for good."

I tugged her hand. She followed me down the hall.

"But — how?" she asked.

Stepping into my room, we both cried out at once.

We heard a final kick — and the closet door swung open.

Slappy burst out, his eyes wild with rage. "Guess what, slaves?" he rasped. "Slappy wins!"

"Grab him!" I cried to my sister.

I reached out both arms and made a frantic dive for the dummy. But he scampered to the side and slipped away from my tackle.

His blue eyes flashed excitedly. His red lips twisted in an ugly grin.

"Give up, slaves!" he rasped. "You cannot win!"

Sara held back, hands against the door frame. I could see the fear in her eyes.

I made another grab for Slappy. Missed again.

"Sara — help me!" I pleaded.

Sara took a step into the room.

I leaped at Slappy, grabbed one boneless ankle.

With a grunt, he pulled out of my grasp. He darted toward the door — and ran right into Sara.

The collision stunned them both.

Sara staggered back.

Slappy teetered off balance.

I threw myself at him, caught his arms, and pulled them behind his back.

He squirmed and twisted. He kicked out furiously.

But Sara grabbed both of his big leather shoes. "Tie him in a knot!" she cried breathlessly.

He kicked and thrashed.

But we held tight.

I twisted his arms behind him. Twisted them around each other. Twisted. Twisted. Then tied them in as tight a knot as I could.

Slappy squirmed and bucked, grunting loudly, his wooden jaws clicking.

When I glanced up from my work on the arms, I saw that Sara had wrapped his legs in a knot, too.

Slappy tilted back his head and uttered a roar of rage. His eyes slid up into his head so that only the whites showed. *Put me down, slaves! Put me down at once!*"

With one hand, I grabbed a wad of tissues from my bed table and jammed it into Slappy's mouth.

He uttered a grunt of protest, then went silent.

"Now what?" Sara cried breathlessly. "Where should we put him?"

My eyes shot around the room. *No*, I decided. *I don't want him in my room. I don't want him in the house.*

"Outside," I instructed my sister, holding on to the knotted arms with both of my hands. "Let's get him outside."

Struggling to hold on to the bucking legs, Sara glanced at the clock. "It's after eleven. What if Mom and Dad hear us?"

"I don't care!" I cried. "Hurry! I want him out of here! I never want to see him again!"

We dragged Slappy out into the hall. Mom and Dad's door remained closed.

Good, I thought. They hadn't heard our struggle.

Sara carried him by the knotted legs. I held on to the arms.

Slappy had stopped struggling and squirming. I think he was waiting to see what we were going to do with him. The wad of tissues had silenced his cries.

I didn't know where to take him. I only knew I wanted him out of the house.

We carried him through the darkened living room and out the front door. We stepped into a hot, sticky night, more like summer than spring. A pale sliver of a moon hovered low in a blue-black sky.

There was no breeze. No sounds of any kind. Nothing moved.

Sara and I carried the dummy to the driveway. "Should we take him somewhere on our bikes?" she suggested.

"How will we balance him?" I asked. "Besides,

it's too dark. Too dangerous. Let's just carry him a few blocks and dump him somewhere."

"You mean in a trash can or something?" Sara asked.

I nodded. "That's where he belongs. In the trash."

Luckily, the dummy didn't weigh much at all. We made our way to the sidewalk, then carried him to the end of the block.

Slappy remained limp, his eyes rolled up in his head.

At the corner, I spotted two circles of white light approaching. Car headlights. "Quick!" I whispered to Sara.

We slipped behind a hedge just in time. The car rolled by without slowing.

We waited for the glow of red taillights to disappear in the darkness. Then we continued down the next block, carrying the dummy between us.

"Hey — how about those?" Sara asked, pointing with her free hand.

I squinted to see what she had spotted. A row of metal trash cans lined up at the curb in front of a dark house across the street.

"Looks good," I said. "Let's shove him in and clamp down the lid. Maybe the trash guys will haul him away tomorrow."

I led the way across the street — and then stopped. "Sara — wait," I whispered. "I have a better idea."

I dragged the dummy toward the corner. I motioned to the metal drain down at the curb.

"The sewer?" Sara whispered.

I nodded. "It's perfect." Through the narrow opening at the curb, I could hear running water far down below. "Come on. Shove him in."

Slappy still didn't move or protest in any way.

I lowered his head to the drain opening. Then Sara and I pushed him in headfirst.

I heard a *splash* and a hard *thud* as he hit the sewer floor.

We both listened. Silence. Then the soft trickle of water.

Sara and I grinned at each other.

We hurried home. I was so happy, I skipped most of the way.

The next morning, Sara and I came to the kitchen for breakfast together. Mom turned from the counter, where she was pouring herself a cup of coffee.

Jed was already at the table, eating his Frosted Flakes. "What's *he* doing down here?" Jed asked.

He pointed across the table.

At Slappy. Sitting in the chair.

Sara and I both gasped.

"Yes. Why is that dummy down here?" Mom asked me. "I found him sitting there when I came in this morning. And why is he so dirty? Where has he been, Amy?"

I could barely choke out a word. "I . . . uh . . . I guess he fell or something," I finally mumbled.

"Well, take him back upstairs," Mom ordered. "He's supposed to be kept in the closet — remember?"

"Uh . . . yeah. I remember," I said, sighing.

"You'll have to clean him up later," Mom said, stirring her coffee. "He looks as if he's been wallowing in the mud."

"Okay," I replied weakly.

I hoisted Slappy up and slung him over my shoulder. Then I started to my room.

"I — I'll come with you," Sara stammered.

"What for?" Mom demanded. "Sit down, Sara, and eat your breakfast. You're both going to be late."

Sara obediently sat down across from Jed. I made my way down the hall.

I was halfway to my room when Slappy raised his head and whispered in my ear, "Good morning, slave. Did you sleep well?"

I tossed him into the closet and locked the door. I could hear him laughing inside the closet. The evil laugh made me shake all over.

What am I going to do now? I asked myself. *What can I do to get rid of this creature?*

The day dragged by. I don't think I heard a word my teacher said.

I couldn't get Slappy's evil, grinning face out of my mind. His raspy voice rattled in my ears.

I won't be your slave! I silently vowed. *I'll get you out of my house — out of my life — if it's the last thing I do!*

That night, I lay wide awake in my bed. How could I sleep, knowing that evil dummy sat in the closet a few feet away?

The night was hot and steamy. I had pushed the window open all the way, but there was no breeze. A fly buzzed by my head, the first fly of spring.

Staring up at the twisting shadows on the ceiling, I brushed the fly away with one hand. As soon as the buzzing vanished, another sound took its place.

113

A click. A low squeak.

The sound of the closet door opening.

I raised myself up off the pillow. Squinting into the darkness, I saw Slappy creep out of the closet.

He took a few shuffling steps, his big shoes sliding silently over my carpet. He turned.

Was he coming toward my bed?

No.

His head and shoulders bobbed as he pulled himself to the door. Then out into the hall.

He's going to Sara's room, I knew.

But what was he going to do there? Did he plan to pay us back for what we did to him last night?

What new horror was he going to create?

I lowered my feet to the floor, climbed out of bed, and followed him out into the hall.

My eyes adjusted quickly to the dim yellow light from the night-light at the other end of the hall. I watched Slappy slither toward my sister's room. He moved as silently as a shadow.

I held my breath and kept my back against the wall as I followed behind him. When he turned into Sara's room, I stepped away from the wall and started to run.

I reached the bedroom doorway in time to see Slappy pick up a wide paintbrush from Sara's supply table. He took a step toward the mural on the wall.

One step.

And then another small figure leaped out of the darkness.

The lights flashed on.

"Dennis!" I cried.

"*Stand back!*" Dennis ordered in a high, shrill voice. He lowered his wooden head and charged at Slappy.

Sara sat up in her bed and uttered a frightened cry.

I could see the stunned expression on Slappy's face.

Dennis flew at Slappy. He slammed his head into Slappy's middle.

Slappy let out a loud *"Oooof!"* He staggered back. Fell.

A loud *thud* rang through the room as the back of Slappy's head hit Sara's iron bedpost.

I raised both hands to my cheeks and gasped as Slappy's head cracked open.

The wooden head split down the middle.

I watched the evil face crack apart. The wide, shocked eyes slid in different directions. The red lips cracked and fell away.

The head dropped to the floor in two pieces. And then the body collapsed in a heap beside them.

My hands still pressed against my face, my heart pounding, I took a few steps into the room.

Dennis ran past me, out to the hall.

But my eyes were locked on the two pieces of Slappy's head. I stared in horror as an enormous white worm crawled out of one of the pieces. The fat worm slithered and curled to the wall — and vanished into a crack in the molding.

Sara climbed out of bed, breathing hard, her face bright red from the excitement.

The closet door swung open. Mom and Dad

came bursting out.

"Girls — are you okay?" Dad cried.

We nodded.

"We saw the whole thing!" Mom exclaimed. She threw her arms around me. "Amy, I'm so sorry. I'm so sorry. We should have believed you. I'm so sorry we didn't believe you."

"We believe you now!" Dad declared, staring down at Slappy's broken head, his crumpled body. "We saw everything!"

It was all planned. Sara and I had worked it out before dinner.

Sara convinced Mom and Dad to hide in the closet. Mom and Dad were really creeped out by the way I was acting. They were willing to do anything.

So Sara pretended to go to sleep. Mom and Dad hid in the closet.

I left the closet door unlocked to make it easier for Slappy to get out.

I knew Slappy would creep into Sara's room. I knew Mom and Dad would finally see that I'm not crazy.

And then Jed burst out dressed as Dennis, with Dennis's head propped up on top of his turtleneck sweater.

We knew that would shock Slappy. We knew it would give us a chance to grab him.

We didn't know what a great job Jed would do. We didn't know that Jed would actually destroy the evil dummy. We didn't know that

Slappy's head would crack apart. That was just good luck.

"Hey — where *is* Jed?" I asked, my eyes searching the room.

"Jed? Jed?" Mom called. "Where are you? You did a great job!"

No reply.

No sign of my brother.

"Weird," Sara muttered, shaking her head.

We all trooped down the hall into Jed's room.

We found him in bed, sound asleep. He groggily raised his head from the pillow and squinted at us. "What time is it?" he asked sleepily.

"It's nearly eleven," Dad replied.

"Oh, no!" Jed cried, sitting up. "I'm sorry! I forgot to wake up! I forgot I was supposed to dress up like Dennis!"

I felt a shiver run down my back. I turned to my parents. "Then who fought Slappy?" I asked. "Who fought Slappy?"

About the Author

R.L. Stine's books are read all over the world. So far, his books have sold more than 300 million copies, making him one of the most popular children's authors in history. Besides Goosebumps, R.L. Stine has written the teen series Fear Street. R.L. Stine lives in New York with his wife, Jane, and Minnie, his King Charles spaniel. You can learn more about him at www.RLStine.com.

Turn the page for a peek at the next
all-terrifying thrill ride from R.L. Stine.

I went invisible for the first time on my twelfth birthday.

It was all Whitey's fault, in a way. Whitey is my dog. He's just a mutt, part terrier, part everything else. He's all black, so of course we named him Whitey.

If Whitey hadn't been sniffing around in the attic . . .

Well, maybe I'd better back up a bit and start at the beginning.

My birthday was on a rainy Saturday. It was a few minutes before kids would start arriving for my birthday party, so I was getting ready.

Getting ready means brushing my hair.

My brother is always on my case about my hair. He gives me a hard time because I spend so much time in front of the mirror brushing it and checking it out.

The thing is, I just happen to have great hair. It's very thick and sort of a golden brown, and just a little bit wavy. My hair is my best feature, so I like to make sure it looks okay.

Also, I have very big ears. They stick out a lot. So I have to keep making sure that my hair covers my ears. It's important.

"Max, it's messed up in back," my brother, Lefty, said, standing behind me as I studied my hair in the front hall mirror.

His name is really Noah, but I call him Lefty because he's the only left-handed person in our family. Lefty was tossing a softball up and catching it in his left hand. He knew he wasn't supposed to toss that softball around in the house, but he always did it anyway.

Lefty is two years younger than me. He's not a bad guy, but he has too much energy. He always has to be tossing a ball around, drumming his hands on the table, hitting something, running around, falling down, leaping into things, wrestling with me. You get the idea. Dad says that Lefty has ants in his pants. It's a dumb expression, but it sort of describes my brother.

I turned and twisted my neck to see the back of my hair. "It is *not* messed up, liar," I said.

"Think fast!" Lefty shouted, and he tosssed the softball at me.

I made a grab for it and missed. It hit the wall just below the mirror with a loud *thud*. Lefty and I held our breath, waiting to see if Mom heard the sound. But she didn't. I think she was in the kitchen doing something to the birthday cake.

"That was dumb," I whispered to Lefty. "You almost broke the mirror."

"*You're* dumb," he said. Typical.

"Why don't you learn to throw right-handed? Then maybe I could catch it sometimes," I told him. I liked to tease him about being left-handed because he really hated it.

"You stink," he said, picking up the softball.

I was used to it. He said it a hundred times a day. I guess he thought it was clever or something.

He's a good kid for a ten-year-old, but he doesn't have much of a vocabulary.

"Your ears are sticking out," he said.

I knew he was lying. I started to answer him, but the doorbell rang.

He and I raced down the narrow hallway to the front door. "Hey, it's *my* party!" I told him.

But Lefty got to the door first and pulled it open.

My best friend, Zack, pulled open the screen door and hurried into the house. It was starting to rain pretty hard, and he was already soaked.

He handed me a present, wrapped in silver paper, raindrops dripping off it. "It's a bunch of comic books," he said. "I already read 'em. The *X-Force* graphic novel is kind of cool."

"Thanks," I said. "They don't look too wet."

Lefty grabbed the present from my hand and ran into the living room with it. "Don't open it!"

I shouted. He said he was just starting a pile.

Zack took off his Red Sox cap, and I got a look at his new haircut. "Wow! You look . . . different," I said, studying his new look. His black hair was buzzed real short on the left side. The rest of it was long, brushed straight to the right.

"Did you invite girls?" he asked me, "or is it just boys?"

"Some girls are coming," I told him. "Erin and April. Maybe my cousin Debra." I knew he liked Debra.

He nodded thoughtfully. Zack has a real serious face. He has these little blue eyes that always look faraway, like he's thinking hard about something. Like he's real deep.

He's sort of an intense guy. Not nervous. Just keyed up. And very competitive. He has to win at everything. If he comes in second place, he gets really upset and kicks the furniture. You know the kind.

"What are we going to do?" Zack asked, shaking the water off his Red Sox cap.

I shrugged. "We were supposed to be in the backyard. Dad put the volleyball net up this morning. But that was before it started to rain. I rented some movies. Maybe we'll watch them."

The doorbell rang. Lefty appeared again from out of nowhere, pushed Zack and me out of the way, and made a dive for the door. "Oh, it's you," I heard him say.

"Thanks for the welcome." I recognized Erin's squeaky voice. Some kids call Erin "Mouse" because of that voice, and because she's tiny like a mouse. She has short, straight blond hair, and I think she's cute, but of course I'd never tell anyone that.

"Can we come in?" I recognized April's voice next. April is the other girl in our group. She has curly black hair and dark, sad eyes. I always thought she was really sad, but then I figured out that she's just shy.

"The party's tomorrow," I heard Lefty tell them.

"Huh?" Both girls uttered cries of surprise.

"No, it isn't," I shouted. I stepped into the doorway and shoved Lefty out of the way. I pushed open the screen door so Erin and April could come in. "You know Lefty's little jokes," I said, squeezing my brother against the wall.

"Lefty *is* a little joke," Erin said.

"You're stupid," Lefty told her. I pressed him into the wall a little harder, leaning against him with all my weight. But he ducked down and scooted away.

"Happy birthday," April said, shaking the rain from her curly hair. She handed me a present, wrapped in Christmas wrapping paper. "It's the only paper we had," she explained, seeing me staring at it.

"Merry Christmas to you, too," I joked. The present felt like a CD.

"I forgot your present," Erin said.

"What is it?" I asked, following the girls into the living room.

"I don't know. I haven't bought it yet."

Lefty grabbed April's present out of my hand and ran to put it on top of Zack's present in the corner behind the couch.

Erin plopped down on the white leather ottoman in front of the armchair. April stood at the window, staring out at the rain.

"We were going to barbecue hot dogs," I said.

"They'd be pretty soggy today," April replied.

Lefty stood behind the couch, tossing his softball up and catching it one-handed.

"You're going to break that lamp," I warned him.

He ignored me, of course.

"Who else is coming?" Erin asked.

Before I could answer, the doorbell rang again. Lefty and I raced to the door. He tripped over his own sneakers and went skidding down the hall on his stomach. So typical.

By two-thirty everyone had arrived, fifteen kids in all, and the party got started. Well, it didn't really get started because we couldn't decide what to do. I wanted to watch a *Terminator* movie. But the girls wanted to play Twister.

"It's *my* birthday!" I insisted.

We compromised. We played Twister. Then we watched some of the *Terminator* movie until it was time to eat.

It was a pretty good party. I think everyone had an okay time. Even April seemed to be having fun. She was usually really quiet and nervous-looking at parties.

Lefty spilled his Coke and ate his slice of chocolate birthday cake with his hands because he thought it was funny. But he was the only animal in the group.

I told him the only reason he was invited was because he was in the family and there was nowhere else we could stash him. He replied by opening his mouth up real wide so everyone could see his chewed-up chocolate cake inside.

After I opened presents, I put the *Terminator* movie back on. But everyone started to leave. I guess it was about five o'clock. It looked much later. It was dark as night out, still storming.

My parents were in the kitchen cleaning up. Erin and April were the only ones left. Erin's mother was supposed to pick them up. She called and said she'd be a little late.

Whitey was standing at the living room window, barking his head off. I looked outside. I didn't see anyone there. I grabbed him with both hands and wrestled him away from the window.

"Let's go up to my room," I suggested when I finally got the dumb dog quiet. "I got a new video game I want to try."

Erin and April gladly followed me upstairs.

They didn't like the movie, for some reason.

The upstairs hallway was pitch black. I clicked the light switch, but the overhead light didn't come on. "The bulb must be burned out," I said.

My room was at the end of the hall. We made our way slowly through the darkness.

"It's kind of spooky up here," April said quietly.

And just as she said it, the linen closet door swung open and, with a deafening howl, a dark figure leapt out at us.

As the girls cried out in horror, the howling creature grabbed me around the waist and wrestled me to the floor.

"Lefty — *let go!*" I screamed angrily. "You're not funny!"

He was laughing like a lunatic. He thought he was a riot. "Gotcha!" he cried. "I gotcha good!"

"We weren't scared," Erin insisted. "We knew it was you."

"Then why'd you scream?" Lefty asked.

Erin didn't have an answer.

I shoved him off me and climbed to my feet. "That was dumb, Lefty."

"How long were you waiting in the linen closet?" April asked.

"A long time," Lefty told her. He started to get up, but Whitey ran up to him and began furiously licking his face. It tickled so much, Lefty fell onto his back, laughing.

"You scared Whitey, too," I said.

"No, I didn't. Whitey's smarter than you

guys." Lefty pushed Whitey away.

Whitey began sniffing at the door across the hall.

"Where does that door lead, Max?" Erin asked.

"To the attic," I told her.

"You have an attic?" Erin cried. Like it was some kind of big deal. "What's up there? I *love* attics!"

"Huh?" I squinted at her in the dark. Sometimes girls are really weird. I mean, how could anyone *love* attics?

"Just a lot of old junk my grandparents left," I told her. "This house used to be theirs. Mom and Dad stored a lot of their stuff in the attic. We hardly ever go up there."

"Can we go up and take a look?" Erin asked.

"I guess," I said. "I don't think it's too big a thrill or anything."

"I love old junk," Erin said.

"But it's so dark. . . ." April said softly. I think she was a little scared.

I opened the door and reached for the light switch just inside. A ceiling light clicked on in the attic. It cast a pale yellow light down at us as we stared up the steep wooden stairs.

"See? There's light up there," I told April. I started up the stairs. They creaked under my sneakers. My shadow was really long. "You coming?"

"Erin's mom will be here any minute,"

April said.

"We'll just go up for a second," Erin said. She gave April a gentle push. "Come on."

Whitey trotted past us as we climbed the stairs, his tail wagging excitedly, his toenails clicking loudly on the wooden steps. About halfway up, the air grew hot and dry.

I stopped on the top step and looked around. The attic stretched on both sides. It was one long room, filled with old furniture, cardboard cartons, old clothes, fishing rods, stacks of yellowed magazines — all kinds of junk.

"Ooh, it smells so musty," Erin said, moving past me and taking a few steps into the vast space. She took a deep breath. "I love that smell!"

"You're definitely weird," I told her.

Rain drummed loudly against the roof. The sound echoed through the low room, a steady roar. It sounded as if we were inside a waterfall.

All four of us began walking around, exploring. Lefty kept tossing his softball up against the ceiling rafters, then catching it as it came down. I noticed that April stayed close to Erin. Whitey was sniffing furiously along the wall.

"Think there are mice up here?" Lefty asked, a devilish grin crossing his face. I saw April's eyes go wide. "Big fat mice who like to climb up girls' legs?" Lefty teased.

My kid brother has a great sense of humor.

"Could we go now?" April asked impatiently. She started back toward the stairway.

"Look at these old magazines," Erin exclaimed, ignoring her. She picked one up and started flipping through it. "Check this out. The clothes these models are wearing are a riot!"

"Hey — what's Whitey doing?" Lefty asked suddenly.

I followed his gaze to the far wall. Behind a tall stack of cartons, I could see Whitey's tail wagging. And I could hear him scratching furiously at something.

"Whitey — come!" I commanded.

Of course he ignored me. He began scratching harder.

"Whitey, what are you scratching at?"

"Probably pulling a mouse apart," Lefty suggested.

"I'm outta here!" April exclaimed.

"Whitey?" I called. Stepping around an old dining room table, I made my way across the cluttered attic. I quickly saw that he was scratching at the bottom of a door.

"Hey, look!" I called to the others. "Whitey found a hidden door."

"Cool!" Erin cried, hurrying over. Lefty and April were right behind.

"I didn't know this was up here," I said.

"We've got to check it out," Erin urged. "Let's see what's on the other side."

And that's when the trouble all began.

You can understand why I say it was all Whitey's fault, right? If that dumb dog hadn't started sniffing and scratching there, we might never have found the hidden attic room.

And we never would have discovered the exciting — and frightening — secret behind that wooden door.

"Whitey!" I knelt down and pulled the dog away from the door. "What's your problem, doggie?"

As soon as I moved him aside, Whitey lost all interest in the door. He trotted off and started sniffing another corner. Talk about your short attention span. But I guess that's the difference between dogs and people.

The rain continued to pound down, a steady roar just above our heads. I could hear the wind whistling around the corner of the house. It was a real spring storm.

The door had a rusted latch about halfway up. It slid off easily, and the warped wooden door started to swing open before I even pulled at it.

The door hinges squeaked as I pulled the door toward me, revealing solid darkness on the other side.

Before I had gotten the door open halfway, Lefty scooted under me and darted into the dark room.

"*A dead body!*" he shrieked.

"Noooo!" April and Erin both cried out with squeals of terror.

But I knew Lefty's dumb sense of humor. "Nice try, Lefty," I said, and followed him through the doorway.

Of course he was just goofing.

I found myself in a small, windowless room. The only light came from the pale yellow ceiling light behind us in the center of the attic.

"Push the door all the way open so the light can get in," I instructed Erin. "I can't see a thing in here."

Erin pushed open the door and slid a carton over to hold it in place. Then she and April crept in to join Lefty and me.

"It's too big to be a closet," Erin said, her voice sounding even squeakier than usual. "So what is it?"

"Just a room, I guess," I said, still waiting for my eyes to adjust to the dim light.

I took another step into the room. And as I did, a dark figure stepped toward me.

I screamed and jumped back.

The other person jumped back, too.

"It's a mirror, dork!" Lefty said, and started to laugh.

Instantly, all four of us were laughing. Nervous, high-pitched laughter.

It *was* a mirror in front of us. In the pale yellow light filtering into the small, square room,

I could see it clearly now.

It was a big, rectangular mirror, about two feet taller than me, with a dark wood frame. It rested on a wooden base.

I moved closer to it and my reflection moved once again to greet me. To my surprise, the reflection was clear. No dust on the glass, despite the fact that no one had been in here in ages.

I stepped in front of it and started to check out my hair.

I mean, that's what mirrors are for, right?

"Who would put a mirror in a room all by itself?" Erin asked. I could see her dark reflection in the mirror, a few feet behind me.

"Maybe it's a valuable piece of furniture or something," I said, reaching into my jeans pocket for my comb. "You know. An antique."

"Did your parents put it up here?" Erin asked.

"I don't know," I replied. "Maybe it belonged to my grandparents. I just don't know." I ran the comb through my hair a few times.

"Can we go now? This isn't too thrilling," April said. She was still lingering reluctantly in the doorway.

"Maybe it was a carnival mirror," Lefty said, pushing me out of the way and making faces into the mirror, bringing his face just inches from the glass. "You know. One of those fun house mirrors that makes your body look like it's shaped like an egg."

"You're already shaped like an egg," I joked, pushing him aside. "At least, your head is."

"You're a *rotten* egg," he snapped back. "You stink."

I peered into the mirror. I looked perfectly normal, not distorted at all. "Hey, April, come in," I urged. "You're blocking most of the light."

"Can't we just leave?" she asked, whining. Reluctantly, she moved from the doorway, taking a few small steps into the room. "Who cares about an old mirror, anyway?"

"Hey, look," I said, pointing. I had spotted a light attached to the top of the mirror. It was oval-shaped, made of brass or some other kind of metal. The bulb was long and narrow, almost like a fluorescent bulb, only shorter.

I gazed up at it, trying to figure it out in the dim light. "How do you turn it on, I wonder."

"There's a chain," Erin said, coming up beside me.

Sure enough, a slender chain descended from the right side of the lamp, hanging down about a foot from the top of the mirror.

"Wonder if it works," I said.

"The bulb's probably dead," Lefty remarked. Good old Lefty. Always an optimist.

"Only one way to find out," I said. Standing on tiptoes, I stretched my hand up to the chain.

"Be careful," April warned.

"Huh? It's just a light," I told her.

Famous last words.

I reached up. Missed. Tried again. I grabbed the chain on the second try and pulled.

The light came on with a startlingly bright flash. Then it dimmed down to normal light. Very white light that reflected brightly in the mirror.

"Hey — that's better!" I exclaimed. "It lights up the whole room. Pretty bright, huh?"

No one said anything.

"I *said*, pretty bright, huh?"

Still silence from my companions.

I turned around and was surprised to find looks of horror on all three faces.

"Max?" Lefty cried, staring hard at me, his eyes practically popping out of his head.

"Max — where are you?" Erin cried. She turned to April. "Where'd he go?"

"I'm right here," I told them. "I haven't moved."

"But we can't see you!" April cried.